The Thieves
– of –
Tyburn Square

Trailblazer Books

Also by Dave and Neta Jackson

*Hero Tales: A Family Treasury of True Stories
From the Lives of Christian Heroes (Volumes 1 & 2)*

TheThieves
– of –
Tyburn Square

Dave & Neta Jackson

Illustrated by Julian Jackson

BETHANY HOUSE PUBLISHERS
MINNEAPOLIS, MINNESOTA 55438

Inside illustration by Julian Jackson.
Cover design and illustration by Catherine Reishus McLaughlin.

Published by Bethany House Publishers
A Ministry of Bethany Fellowship, Inc.
11300 Hampshire Ave. South
Minneapolis, Minnesota 55438

Printed in the United States of America

Library of Congress Cataloging-in-Publication Data

Jackson, Dave.
    The thieves of Tyburn Square / Dave and Neta Jackson.
       p. cm.
    Summary: In 1817 a teenage brother and sister are relieved from the
abuses of Newgate Prison in London by the prison reform efforts of Quaker
minister Elizabeth Fry.
    ISBN 1–55661–470–5
    1. Fry, Elizabeth Gurney, 1780–1845—Juvenile Fiction. [1. Fry,
Elizabeth Gurney, 1780—1845—Fiction. 2. Newgate (Prison : London,
England)—Fiction. 3. Reformers—Fiction. 4. Quakers—Fiction.
5. Brothers and sisters—Fiction. 6. Christian life—Fiction.] I. Jackson,
Neta. II. Title.
PZ7.J132418TI   1995
[Fic]—dc20   95–43826
                                            CIP
                                            AC

This story covers the year 1817 when Elizabeth Fry began visiting Newgate Prison on a regular basis. During that period, she started the Newgate School and developed meaningful work for women prisoners.

Loren and Betsey Maxwell are fictional characters whose plight is typical of that of slum dwellers in early nineteenth-century London. The same is true of Flori Alexander and several other named prisoners. However, Mary Conner is a true character; she was imprisoned for stealing a watch, became the first schoolmistress of Newgate School, and was later pardoned but died of consumption (tuberculosis) before being released.

The shelter for "vicious and neglected girls" was not begun until 1824, but was moved up in time for the purposes of our story.

DAVE AND NETA JACKSON are a husband/wife writing team who have authored or coauthored many books on marriage and family, the church, and relationships, including the books accompanying the Secret Adventures video series, the Pet Parables series, and the Caring Parent series.

They have three children: Julian, the illustrator for the Trailblazer series, Rachel, a college student, and Samantha, their Cambodian foster daughter. They make their home in Evanston, Illinois, where they are active members of Reba Place Church.

CONTENTS

Chapter 1

The Convict Ship

BETSEY MAXWELL WEARILY TRAILED behind Loren as her brother dodged the muddy puddles, horse manure, and piles of crates in the narrow London street. Her feet were already cold and wet as water seeped through the holes of her thin leather shoes.

"Hurry up, Betsey!" Loren urged, grabbing her hand. "We're almost at the docks. We gotta get there before they bring the prisoners." Loren was twelve— two years older than Betsey. It had been his idea to come to the docks along the River Thames this morning to try to see their mother.

Betsey tried to hurry. But a terrible dread in the pit of her stomach made her want to turn and run back the other way. It had been four months since she'd seen her mother. *All because of that stupid silver candle-stick!* Betsey thought fiercely.

She wished Mama had never gone to that fancy house on Fleet Street to collect the washing. Taking in washing was how Mama tried to make a living, and the people in the fancy house were new customers. But the first time Mama had delivered the basket of freshly scrubbed sheets, pillow covers, and underclothes to Fleet Street, the housekeeper sniffed that the clothes weren't done properly and refused to pay her.

Mrs. Maxwell had climbed the rickety stairs to their two tiny rooms in the crowded tenement house muttering angrily, "Ain't gonna let them rich snobs rob my babies." Betsey noticed her mother was carrying something wrapped in her shawl. She quickly stuffed the package under her mattress. Late that evening, loud shouts and rough laughter from the gin house next door woke Betsey, and she saw her mother slip out into the noisy night with the shawl-wrapped bundle.

But Mama never came home. Instead, a clergyman dressed all in black knocked on their door the next day and told Loren and Betsey that a thief-catcher had caught their mother trying to pawn a stolen candle-stick, and she'd been taken to Newgate Prison.

The clergyman had wanted to take the children to the parish workhouse to await their mother's fate, but Mrs. Hinkley, their upstairs neighbor—a loud woman with painted eyes and red lips who usually slept all day and was out all night—had hotly protested and taken the children up to her own flat. That night a frightened Betsey had cried herself to sleep, huddled on a lumpy straw tick with Mrs. Hinkley's three runny-nosed children. What was going to happen to Mama? What was going to happen to her and Loren?

That was four months ago. Only last week Mrs. Hinkley had gone to the prison and discovered that Kate Maxwell had already been tried and sentenced to "transportation."

"Transportation? You mean . . . she's being exiled to Botany Bay?" Loren had said, his face white under the shock of unruly brown hair.

"Yeah," said Mrs. Hinkley, slumping into a chair by a rough wooden table and uncorking a half-empty bottle of gin. "Better than hangin'," she'd muttered, more to herself than to the frightened children.

Somehow Loren had found out when the prisoners who had been sentenced to "transportation" were being taken from Newgate Prison down to the "convict ships" for their long voyage to Botany Bay. Botany Bay was the place England sent its "criminal class"—a dreaded destination in that wild land called New South Wales on the other side of the world. (New South Wales was a territory on the continent later known as Australia.)

But now as Loren pulled his sister along the docks flanking the River Thames, Betsey's mouth dropped open in dismay. She had thought there would be just one ship at the dock. But a whole row of sailing ships with their tall masts and webs of rigging were moored to the docks with long, heavy ropes. Several more ships were anchored out in the middle of the river. Dockhands were busy loading barrels, live animals, and crates onto some ships and unloading others. Soldiers in bright red coats were saying goodbye to mothers and sweethearts before boarding several troop ships bound for Europe, where the English and their allies were fighting the feisty little French emperor, Napoleon.

"Oh, Loren!" Betsey cried. "How will we ever know which ship they're to put Mama on?"

Loren didn't answer because just then a shout went up from the deck of one of the ships. "Look out, mates! Here they come!" Turning their heads in the direction the deckhand was pointing, Loren and Betsey saw a large, noisy crowd of people coming toward the docks.

"Come on," Loren hissed, pulling Betsey to a spot where the crowd would have to pass them. As the throng came closer they saw not one, but many open wagons, some filled with women, others with men. Running alongside were men, women, and children shouting and jeering at the wagon's occupants.

"Thieves and scoundrels, the lot o' ya!"

"Ha, ha! Good riddance, I say!"

"That's right. Get rid of the criminal class in England. Send 'em all to Botany Bay!"

"Want some food for the voyage, dearie? Here!" A rotten tomato sailed through the air and landed—

splat!—right on the ear of an angry female prisoner.

The occupants of the wagons weren't quiet, either. Shackled together with chains, many of them yelled back at their tormentors, spitting and cursing.

The first wagon of women went by so fast and the crowd around it was so thick that Betsey didn't get a good look. "Did you see her, Loren?" she asked anxiously. Loren didn't answer. He was busy scanning the coming wagons.

"There she is!" he finally cried, pointing to a wagon crammed with women prisoners. "See her, Betsey?" Loren grabbed his younger sister around the waist and lifted her up to see over the crowd.

Betsey's heart was pounding beneath her gray shift and pinafore. At first she couldn't tell which one was Mama. Then she saw Kate Maxwell, looking frightened and bewildered at the crowd of people yelling and jeering all around her.

"Mama!" Betsey screamed. "Mama! Over here!"

But Mrs. Maxwell just stared straight ahead as if she hadn't heard . . . and in the next moment the wagon rumbled out onto the docks.

"Come on," Loren commanded, once again grabbing Betsey's hand and running after the wagon. The two children tried to keep up, but they had to dodge this way and that to keep from being knocked down by the unruly crowd. The wagons carrying the women prisoners had pulled up beside one of the ships swaying gently at the riverside dock; the wagons carrying men and boys rattled on down the docks to another ship farther away.

By the time Loren and Betsey pushed their way
through the crowd, the first wagons of women had

been emptied and the prisoners were being led up the gangplank onto the decks. Frantic, Betsey scanned the figures of the women going on board.

"Mama!" she screamed, hoping her mama would hear. "Mama!" Several women turned to look at her— was one of them Mama? Yes! There she was. She was looking . . . looking—but just then the line of women stepped off the gangplank and disappeared behind the tall bulwarks surrounding the ship's decks.

The heckles of the rowdy crowd still filled the air.

"Transportation's too good for that lot," complained a raspy voice. "Shoulda hung 'em all, if ya ask me."

"Oh, I don' know," said another. "I heard that Botany Bay is the gateway to a living hell."

"Yeah, heh, heh. Full o' savages with spears an' dry, hot desert as far as the eye can see . . ."

Hot tears sprang to Betsey's eyes. Why were the people so mean? Why was the judge sending her mother away? Would she ever see her again? And what were she and Loren going to do now?

Just then a hand touched her shoulder. Startled, Betsey looked up into the face of a woman. "Is thy mother going on that ship?" the woman asked gently.

Instinctively, Betsey shrank away and stared. The woman was wearing a plain black dress and matching cloak, but they rustled as if they were made of silk. Kind gray eyes peered out from under a black bonnet, which framed a pleasant face.

"It's none of your business!" Loren snapped, stepping between his sister and the strange woman.

"Please," the woman said, "I don't mean thee any harm—"

"Come, come, Elizabeth," said a man's voice. Betsey realized the woman was accompanied by a man also dressed plainly in black stockings and breeches and a long, well-made black coat.

"But, Joseph!" the woman cried. "I had no idea such things went on in our own city. Mothers torn away from their children, citizens harassing these unfortunate prisoners who may never see their loved ones again. When Friend Grellet told me to witness the transportation of women prisoners for myself—"

"I know, Elizabeth," the man said quietly. "It is very distressing. But thee can't do anything here. It's out of thy hands for the moment. Come."

Betsey watched as the man led the woman away. She continued to look back over her shoulder at the children. Betsey was sorry she and Loren had been so rude. The woman had been the only kind voice in this pushing, shoving, jeering crowd.

Just then another raspy and mocking voice caught her ear. "Heh, heh. Did ya hear that, Pigeye? Tsk, tsk. Those high 'n mighty Quakers think shipping this criminal cargo to Purgatory is 'so distressing.'"

Betsey wiped the hot tears from her cheeks and pulled closer to Loren. Two young soldiers lounged a few feet away against a big packing barrel, gaping at Loren and Betsey.

"Huh!" said the one named Pigeye. "They should ship the prisoners' brats to Botany Bay, too. Be done with 'em, once and for all."

"Nah, I got a better idea," said the one with the raspy voice. He pushed himself off the barrel and took a step toward Loren and Betsey. "Them two young'uns ain't got no place to go, now, do they?" he said to his buddy. "Their lowdown mama's on that ship an' ain't comin' back, now, is she? An' that girl is a purty little thing, wouldn't ya say, ol' chap?"

Before the young soldier with the raspy voice could take another step, Loren grabbed Betsey's hand and started running away from the dock. Frightened, Betsey ran hard to keep up, forgetting the sores on her feet caused by her damp, torn shoes. As they dodged another wagon full of arriving prisoners, Betsey looked back over her shoulder. The two young men in red coats were still standing on the dock, laughing heartily, watching them go.

As Loren and Betsey reached the narrow street leading away from the riverside, the boy slowed down, then stopped. He looked back at the row of ships, their masts swaying like a forest of trees in the damp breeze blowing off the River Thames.

"Don't you worry, Betsey," Loren said fiercely, putting an arm awkwardly around his sister's shoulder as they started slowly back toward Mrs. Hinkley's flat. "I'll take care of you—no matter what!"

It was midmorning when the children arrived back at the flat in one of London's slums. They tiptoed up the squeaky stairs and pushed open the door as quietly as possible because Mrs. Hinkley usually slept till noon.

But Mrs. Hinkley had a visitor.

Chapter 2

The Workhouse

BETSEY FELT LOREN STIFFEN. The same clergyman who had brought the message that their mother had been arrested was sitting awkwardly on a wooden chair in the middle of the sparsley furnished room. Mrs. Hinkley, slouching bleary-eyed in the other chair and cradling a bottle of gin, had obviously been awakened too early.

"Are these the children?" the clergyman said, frowning.

Mrs. Hinkley nodded, glaring at Loren and Betsey. "Where 'ave you two been?" she snapped. "What do ya mean runnin' off while I'm sleepin' without tellin' me where yer goin'?"

"We went down to the docks," Loren spoke up. "Wanted to see Mama before—" He stopped.

"We didn't want to wake you," Betsey added anxiously.

Mrs. Hinkley's harsh face, white and thin without the gaudy paints she put on at night when she went out, suddenly crumpled as if she was about to cry. "God 'ave mercy on tha' poor woman," she moaned into her bottle. "An' now what am I gonna do with two orphans, Rev'rend Simpson? Two growin' mouths to feed when I can 'ardly feed my own!"

The clergyman cleared his throat. "That, Mrs. Hinkley, is why I'm here," he said, looking as if he wished he were somewhere else. "I received word from the prison that Mrs. Maxwell has been tried and sentenced to transportation, leaving behind two minor children. It is our duty to see that the children of condemned prisoners within our parish are provided for by relatives, or . . . er . . . proper guardians, or placed in the care of the parish workhouse."

Stunned, Loren and Betsey looked anxiously at Mrs. Hinkley. Mrs. Hinkley had taken them in while Mama was in prison. But would she want to keep them now that their mother was gone for good?

Not that they really *liked* living with Mrs. Hinkley. The flat was small and crowded, and she expected them to keep her three bratty children quiet while she slept in the daytime. Meals were scanty and irregular, mostly bread and tea and sugar; in fact, Mrs. Hinkley never really *cooked* beyond

19

boiling a pot of vegetables flavored with an occasional soupbone. And even though she called herself Mrs. Hinkley, they'd never seen a Mr. Hinkley. But almost every evening she got gussied up in fancy clothes and went out, not returning till three or four in the morning. Betsey thought maybe she was a barmaid. The pubs and taverns—and there were two or three on every street in the slums of London—stayed open till all hours of the night.

The children and Mrs. Hinkley stared at each other for a long minute. Finally Mrs. Hinkley looked away. "I don' like the idea of sendin' innocent children to the workhouse . . ." The woman's voice, thick with gin, trailed off.

"Come, come, Mrs. Hinkley," said Reverend Simpson. "The parish workhouse will keep these youngsters off the street, away from evil influences. Good, hard work will give them discipline, keep their minds and hands busy. Of course, if you want to take on that responsibility yourself, and *legally* become their guardian . . ."

Mrs. Hinkley stood up quickly, almost knocking over the chair. "Eh? *Legal* guardian, you say?" The woman paced nervously back and forth in the small room. "People comin' to check up on me an' mine to see if I'm fit? Pokin' their noses into my business? Oh no, ya don't, Rev'rend Simpson." She waved the gin bottle at the clergyman. "What I do is *my* business, an' I don' want no preacher or sheriff comin' around to check up on me. No, sir."

Mrs. Hinkley suddenly stopped pacing and looked

dully at the Maxwell children. "I wanted to keep you and your sister out of the workhouse, Loren, yes I did. But . . . I can't afford to keep feedin' ya, an' you an' I both know your mama ain't comin' back." She took a long drink from the gin bottle, then wiped her mouth with the back of her hand. "You and your sister pack up your things an' go along with Reverend Simpson. Go on, now."

✧ ✧ ✧ ✧

Reverend Simpson pulled a bell rope outside an iron gate set in a massive stone wall. Betsey strained her neck, but all she could see in any direction were factories belching dark smoke that stung her eyes and nose. The gate soon swung open, and a gateman ushered the trio across a narrow brick courtyard and into a large, gloomy building.

The clergyman spoke in a low voice to the workhouse superintendent, a Mr. Dimmitt, who must have been very hot because the man kept mopping his fat, perspiring face with a large, dirty handkerchief. The superintendent nodded, rang a bell, and before Betsey realized what was happening, a matron in a white cap and pinafore over a gray dress had swished into the office and bundled Betsey off down a narrow hall.

"Wait!" Betsey cried. "We left Loren! I want my brother!"

"Nonsense," said the matron and kept marching. "Your brother can't come on the women's side, now, can he? Men and boys on the east side; women and girls on the west side. That's the way it is at the workhouse."

"But when can I see my brother?" asked Betsey, alarmed. She didn't know what to expect at the workhouse, but she knew she could face whatever it was a lot better if she and Loren could be together.

"You'll see him at mealtimes sitting on the men's side—but there'll be no talking," said the matron sternly. "That's the rule."

Betsey soon learned there were a lot of rules in the workhouse. No talking at meals. No playing. No running. Get up at six. Pass inspection. Breakfast of broth and bread promptly at six-thirty. Work at seven. No talking while working. Dinner of broth and bread at one. Work from one to seven. Supper of potatoes and cabbage. Wash up in cold water. Bed at eight. No talking after eight. If you broke a rule, no dinner. If you talked back to the matron—who was Mr. Dimmitt's wife—you earned a whipping with a hickory stick.

There were two women's dormitories. Betsey slept in a large room with about fifty other women and girls of all ages. Some were ancient grandmothers who could barely get out of bed in the morning and moaned with every step. Some were mere babies, three or four years old, who cried themselves to sleep at night. Betsey longed to take one of the little ones in her arms and comfort her, even though she herself often cried silently until she fell asleep. But that was another rule: no getting out of bed after lights out.

Everyone over eight had to work eleven hours a day. Most of the men and boys worked in one of the nearby factories, most of which were metalworks, tending hot fires which melted iron to make cannonballs and bullets for the war effort against Napoleon, as well as parts for all sorts of newfangled machines. Some of the stronger women and older girls also went to the factories. Others worked the weaving looms, making cheap cloth to be sewn into workhouse clothing; or they scrubbed floors and emptied the slop basins.

When Mrs. Dimmitt, a stiff, humorless woman, learned that Betsey's mother had taken in washing, Betsey was immediately assigned to the crew of women and girls who did all the washing for the workhouse—bedding and towels for two hundred men, women, and children, plus kitchen towels and scrub rags. The work was hard. Everything had to be scrubbed with soap, boiled in big iron pots hanging over open fires in the brick courtyard, then wrung out and hung up to dry. Lice were a constant problem, and a monthly washing of all bedding with caustic lye soap burned big red patches on Betsey's arms and hands.

Like all the other girls and women, Betsey was provided with one dress, a set of underclothes, a pair of stockings, a pair of shoes, and a night shift to sleep in. These personal garments were washed out by hand once every two weeks. And regardless of the original color of the garments, everything was soon reduced to a shade of sooty gray from the relentless smoke-filled air from the factories.

At every meal, Betsey's eyes hunted among the boys for a glimpse of Loren. Sometimes their eyes met, but they didn't dare look for long lest the matron or the superintendent catch them. But Betsey lived for that look, a brief comfort that let her know she wasn't alone in this awful place.

Sometimes at night, she dreamed about that last time she'd seen her mother down at the docks. Such a fleeting glimpse! Each time the dream invaded her sleep, the wagon seemed to fly by faster and her mother's face grew dimmer. But another face stayed clear and distinct: that of the Quaker woman in her black bonnet and black silk dress, saying kindly, "Please, I don't mean thee any harm." *Elizabeth, the man had called her. Elizabeth* . . . Betsey's own name.

✧ ✧ ✧ ✧

The only break in the tedious days was Sunday, when Reverend Simpson or one of his assistant ministers came in the afternoon to read long passages of Scripture and recite monotonous prayers to the residents of the parish workhouse. Weeks piled upon weeks, and month after dreary month added up to years. All that Betsey knew of the passage of time were the damp, chilly winters and the short, warmer summers, when the sun could occasionally be seen through the haze of factory smoke.

And as the seasons passed, Betsey's work assignments changed. She was moved from the laundry to the scullery, washing dishes three times a day for the workhouse residents, whose numbers swelled to three hundred after England and her allies defeated Napoleon at the Battle of Waterloo. Betsey's next job was at the weaving looms, which she liked best of all since the work was dry and her chapped, red hands gradually healed.

But soon after Betsey and Loren's third Christmas in the workhouse—a day marked by nothing more than a much-needed day of rest and a long Christmas sermon by Reverend Simpson—the matron announced that since Betsey was now thirteen, she had a new work assignment: in the metalworks factory along with the older girls.

Betsey's stomach tightened with dread. She had seen the older girls coming back to the workhouse from the factory, their eyes glazed with exhaustion, their clothing and skin covered with burns from the sparks that flew from the molten iron. On the first morning of her new work assignment, however, as she lined up with the others in the brick courtyard, her heart gave a little leap. There on the other side of the courtyard, in the line of men and boys waiting for the iron gate to be unlocked, was Loren.

With a start Betsey realized that her brother was practically a grown man of fifteen now. Seeing him on the way to the factory, Betsey felt a tiny flicker of hope. It would be worth working in the factory if it meant she got to see Loren more often. If only they could find a way to talk to each other!

Just then she caught Loren's eye—but a fierce, angry look clouded her brother's face. He looked away, his eyes narrow and his face hard as the two lines shuffled out the gate toward the factory. Bewildered, Betsey focused on the back of the woman in front of her. Why was Loren angry? Was he angry at her?

Betsey was assigned to haul coal from the big piles against the wall of the factory to the large brick ovens. She could barely lift the heavy bucket with both hands. Half lifting, half dragging, she finally got the bucket to the oven, where it was emptied into the fire in one swoop by a big brawny fire tender and abruptly handed back to her to refill. All day long she hauled coal, her muscles protesting with each trip. By the time the long day was over, Betsey was too tired to even eat her supper of potatoes and cabbage.

The next morning, Betsey could hardly move. As she stood wearily in the line of factory workers, she glanced furtively at the men's line. Was Loren still angry? Maybe he didn't want her looking for him. Still, she couldn't help watching out of the corner of her eye until she found him. The hard, angry look was still there. No, wait—as she caught his eye, his face softened a little bit. A hint of a smile flickered around his mouth before he looked away.

Then Betsey noticed something else. Loren shifted his place in line, and as the two lines filed out the gate, he was only four people ahead of her.

The following day Betsey was so weary, she almost forgot to look for Loren in the courtyard, but as she stumbled toward another long day hauling coal, she realized Loren was only two people ahead of her in the next line. She could almost reach out and touch him—but she didn't dare.

And then, the next day, Betsey found herself walking alongside her brother as the men's line and the women's line plodded wearily to the factory.

Loren didn't look at her. But as the sounds of the factory began to surround them, she heard his voice beside her, low and urgent. "Hold on, Betsey. When Sunday comes, be alert."

Chapter 3

Tyburn Square

BETSEY HAD NO IDEA what day it was. The week had been so long and so hard, one day seemed just like the next—except her muscles were stiffer and sorer each morning when she got out of bed at six o'clock. When was Sunday? Another couple days at least. What did Loren mean, "When Sunday comes, be alert"?

By the time Sunday came, however, Betsey was so tired she didn't really care. All she wanted to do was sleep. While Reverend Simpson was reading a long passage from the book of Jeremiah Sunday afternoon, Betsey's eyes

drooped, then closed . . . and the next thing she knew she'd been thumped on the head by Mr. Dimmitt's cane.

"Disrespectful!" the superintendent hissed. "Sleeping while the Holy Scriptures are read. Wake up, girl, or your soul will be in peril!"

Monday came. A steady drizzle was falling as the factory crews lined up in the courtyard. Betsey's teeth were chattering by the time the iron gate was unlocked and the two lines started moving out into the narrow street and down toward the metalworks factory.

Everyone in the lines was hunched against the cold, wet January day. So no one—not even Betsey—saw Loren pull back his throwing arm and let fly with a rock against a big metal sign hanging over the factory door. Rock against metal had the effect of ringing a gong; startled, the factory workers looked up—a few had to jump out of the way of the offending rock as it fell.

At just that moment, Betsey felt a strong hand grab her arm and pull her out of the line, then push her down behind some large barrels standing outside the factory wall. She almost screamed, but caught herself as Loren's voice hissed, "Shh!"

In the confusion of the clanging sign, no one seemed to notice that Loren and Betsey were missing from the lines. Soon the wet, miserable workers had shuffled inside the factory and the doors were closed.

"Run!" Loren cried, pulling Betsey to her feet and

starting off in the opposite direction from the work-house. *Run?* Betsey's muscles were still so sore, even after a day of rest, she ached just walking. But fear pushed energy into her legs, and she flew after Loren.

This way and that Loren darted through the narrow alleyways of London's slums. He seemed to be going somewhere—but where? Betsey was too out of breath to ask.

Soon the pair slowed down. The morning drizzle had finally stopped, though by this time Betsey's clothes were damp down to her skin. Still, she began to look around curiously. Ladies with baskets were hustling to the shops, holding their long skirts up to avoid the swollen puddles. Street sellers were pushing their carts along the cobblestones, hawking their wares.

"Apples! Apples! Only a ha'penny."

"Knives sharpened! Bring your knives to be sharpened!"

"Jelly tarts! Fresh this mornin'!"

Betsey's mouth watered. As the old familiar sights and sounds of London soaked in, she began to feel like a bird that had flown out of its cage. And it'd been years since she'd seen such a big grin on Loren's face.

"I thought you were angry at me," she told him. "You looked so fierce when I saw you in the courtyard."

"Angry at *you*, Betsey?" Loren said, surprised. "Not you! But I *was* angry when I saw you'd been assigned to the factory. I've seen what it's done to the older girls, how worn out they get, old before their time. That's when I knew it was time."

Betsey pulled Loren to a stop. The long run had given her a stitch in her side. "Time? For what?" she asked, sinking down in a doorway to rest.

Loren looked uneasily up and down the street, then lowered his voice. "I've been planning to run away for a long time, figuring how to do it. I didn't want to go unless we could go together—but they kept us separated all the time, would never let us talk! When I saw you in the factory line, at first I was angry. Then I realized—this was our chance! It meant both of us were going outside the iron gate each day. All I had to do was create a distraction so we could get away."

Sitting in the doorway in her damp clothes, Betsey shivered. "But . . . what are we going to do? We don't have any place to live, or . . . or money to buy food." The first, delicious taste of freedom was slipping away in the reality of being cold and homeless on the streets of London. What if someone caught them and sent them back to the workhouse?

Loren seemed to read her mind. "We'll never go back!" he said fiercely. "Didn't I promise you I would take care of you when Mama got transported? Well, I have a plan. Come on."

He started off again and Betsey reluctantly followed. She'd really rather sit and rest awhile longer. On the other hand, she soon realized, walking made her warmer than sitting in her damp clothes. She gave a couple skips to catch up and decided to enjoy the adventure of being outside the workhouse walls. After all, Loren had a plan, didn't he?

The pair turned down Star Street and soon joined a lighthearted crowd moving in the same direction.

"I see you're goin' to 'Tyburn Fair' this morning, Mrs. Tibbet!" a businessman in a top hat called out to an overdressed woman in stiff skirts, coat, shawl, and parasol who was pulling along a lad of about ten by the coat sleeve.

"Aye, that I am!" said the woman crossly. "An' Tom here is goin', too, so he knows what happens to thieves and liars."

The man chuckled and was soon swallowed up in the crowd, but Betsey noticed that all sorts of people seemed to be going to this Tyburn Fair, whatever that was. Well-dressed businessmen, parents with children, and ladies and gentlemen in fine clothes mixed with shopkeepers in their aprons, day laborers, sailors, and beggars. The mood was high, and the street sellers with their carts of food and drink were doing a brisk business.

"Here," Loren said casually, handing Betsey a warm jelly tart while he bit into another.

Her eyes widened. "Loren Maxwell!" she gasped. "Did you . . . you didn't . . . ?"

Loren grinned. "Naw, I didn't steal 'em. I *paid* for 'em—with this." He tapped a soft leather money pouch tucked into the waist of his trousers.

Betsey hesitated. Where did Loren get a money pouch? But the jelly tart, warm and sticky in her hand, pushed away any nagging thoughts. Loren had paid for it, hadn't he? She bit into the flaky crust, and a burst of warm, fruity sweetness filled her mouth. Oh! She couldn't remember tasting anything so good since . . . since before Mama went away to prison.

The jolly crowd pushed along until Star Street intersected Edgware Road. There the area widened into a sort of public square along the banks of a stream called Ty Bourne. Licking her fingers happily, Betsey happened to look up. Windows in the flats over nearby shops were wide open, and old women and young girls with bare heads leaned out, calling to friends and neighbors they saw in the milling crowd below.

"Who's ridin' the 'three-legged mare' today?" a sassy lass called out boldly from her window perch, pointing to a wooden structure in the center of the square.

"Who cares?" a young man called back. "We're having a grand party so whoever it is can leave this world in style! Come on, tavern keeper—break out that cask of gin!"

As several large casks were rolled out of one of the local pubs to hoots of approval, Betsey looked where the young woman had pointed. A large wooden platform with stairs going up one side stood in the middle of the square. On the platform were three posts linked by crossbars, and hanging from each crossbar was a rope tied into a noose.

So *that* was the "three-legged mare"!

She grabbed Loren's arm. "Loren! Look! It's a

gallows. These people have come to see a hanging!"

Loren frowned and hustled Betsey into an empty doorway. "I know it. Why do you think we came here?"

"But . . . I don't want to see a hanging, Loren! I want to leave—right now." Betsey's heart was pounding anxiously. Why in the world would Loren bring her to Tyburn Square for a public hanging?

"We didn't come to watch the hanging, silly," Loren said impatiently. He looked around and lowered his voice. "I picked up a few tips from the boys in the workhouse," he said, patting the leather pouch in his waist. "A few minutes' quick work in a noisy crowd like this will buy us something to eat and a place by the fire at one of the lodging houses in Chick Lane, that's what. We just have to wait until the wagon from the prison comes and distracts everyone's attention."

Betsey's eyes widened. "Picking people's pockets?" she whispered. "But, Loren, that's—"

Loren's eyes narrowed. "That's the way life is, Betsey," he snapped. "It's living by our wits . . . or the workhouse. Now, what's it gonna be, eh?"

Just then a shout went up. "The wagon's comin'!" The crowd surged forward, then barely parted as a wagon rattled down the street.

Betsey couldn't see what was happening, but the people around her, who were being pushed back by the bailiffs, kept up a running commentary.

"Eh! Two of 'em today! At least they won't be lonely in the netherworld—heh, heh."

"Don't mind so much fer the old man, but t'other one be in his prime."

"So? If they break the law, they gotta pay the price, that's what I say."

Betsey barely realized that Loren was gone before he was back again, slipping something flat and heavy into the pocket of her skirt. "Don't look down—pretend it ain't there," he ordered, then he beckoned to her and they threaded through the crowd, working their way to the other side of the square. "I don't want to be around when that man realizes his wallet is missing," Loren muttered.

Betsey wanted to pull the wallet out of her pocket, throw it down, and run. But she couldn't leave Loren, not after he had risked so much to help her get away from the workhouse. Besides, they needed to stick together if they were going to make it on the streets with no mother, no father, no home. But . . . she felt so confused. Stealing was wrong! And what if they got caught?

Still, maybe Loren was right. It was a matter of survival. How else were they going to buy food to eat or pay for a place to sleep?

By now the fettered prisoners were climbing down from the wagons, accompanied by yells and shouts from the people in the square.

"Stay here," Loren whispered, parking Betsey beside a lamppost. She watched him take a few steps behind a stout gentleman who was cheering the proceedings, lift the man's coattail, and carefully pull out the man's leather wallet from a back pocket.

Swiftly Loren stepped back and slipped the second wallet into the pocket of Betsey's skirt.

But the man must have sensed something was wrong. He patted his empty back pocket and turned in a flash. "My wallet! My wallet's been stolen!" he cried. He caught Loren's eye. "That's the no-good pickpocket! Help! Thief-catcher! Where's the thief-catcher? Stop him!"

Panicked, Betsey was set to flee, but instead of running, Loren stepped away from her and walked directly toward the irate man. "You accuse me, sir? But I don't have your wallet, as you can see." Loren spread his arms innocently, as if to show that he did not have the man's wallet on his person—all the while moving farther away from Betsey so the man's attention would be on him, not her.

The man looked confused. Then he spied the leather coin pouch tucked in Loren's waistband. "Huh! What's a street urchin like you doing with a fine leather pouch like that, eh? Who else did you pickpocket?"

"This pouch?" Loren seemed offended. "Why, it's a gift from my poor, dead father, sir."

Betsey cringed at the lie. Their father had died penniless when she was very small, and she was certain he had never had such a pouch. But Loren's voice was calm and reassuring. "Why would I need to pickpocket anyone when I have my own money pouch?"

Just then Betsey felt a strong hand grab her by the arm. "Here's the boy's accomplice!" bellowed a big voice. "I'll bet my thief-catcher's reward on it."

In a panic, Betsey twisted around and looked up into the leering face of a big, beefy man with bushy eyebrows and an unshaven face. With one hand firmly holding Betsey's arm, the thief-catcher's other hand searched her dress pocket—and pulled out the two fine leather wallets.

Chapter 4

Newgate Prison

MY WALLET!" BELLOWED THE GENTLEMAN. In a flash he grabbed Loren by the collar of his shirt and dragged the boy over to where the thief-catcher was holding a squirming Betsey.

A few people in the crowd glanced at them with mild curiosity, but the attention of most was drawn toward the drama up on the wooden platform.

"Good work, thief-catcher!" puffed the man. "Two wallets, eh? Looks like I'm not the only one being played for a fool by these slum brats. Now, give me my wallet—there, that black one—and you can march these two young thieves to Newgate Prison

and collect your reward."

"Not so fast!" said the thief-catcher, holding the wallets out of reach. "If I give you the wallet, then I won't have proof of their crime now, will I? Nay, you'll have to come along and make your complaint to the magistrate proper-like."

"What?" sputtered the stout gentleman. "I'm a busy man, sir! I don't have time to miss a half day of business because some fool kid tried to lift my wallet. Come, come, be reasonable."

The thief-catcher shrugged. "Well, if you're too busy, I can let the scalawags go—"

"Bah!" cursed the man. Thrusting Loren at the thief-catcher, he turned on his heel and pushed his way through the crowd, heading for Newgate Prison.

❖ ❖ ❖ ❖

The cold, stone walls of Newgate Prison rose high and solid facing Newgate Street. There were no windows or openings, save for an occasional iron grate dotting the wall here and there. The burly thief-catcher pushed Betsey and Loren through the main gate of the prison as they followed the angry gentleman into the admitting room. Betsey shivered as the large wooden doors swung shut behind them. Two bailiffs took charge of Loren and Betsey as the thief-catcher and the gentleman strode up to the magistrate's desk.

Betsey and Loren had not said a word to each other on the long hike from Tyburn Square to

Newgate in the iron grip of the thief-catcher, but now Loren turned to his sister with tortured eyes. "I-I'm sorry, Betsey," he said miserably. "I didn't mean to get you in troub—"

"Silence, rats!" said one of the bailiffs, boxing Loren on the ear so hard the boy fell over.

Frightened tears sprang to Betsey's eyes. What was going to happen to them? Couldn't they just tell the gentleman they were sorry and promise not to steal anymore? She and Loren would just have to think of another way to survive on the streets.

A moment later they were summoned to the desk by the magistrate. "Name and age," the official said in a dry voice.

"Loren Maxwell, fifteen."

"Betsey Maxwell, thirteen."

Scratch, scratch went the quill pen.

The magistrate turned to the gentleman. "You're pressing charges?"

"Of course!" the man snapped, "I wouldn't be wasting my time here, would I? The young scoundrel is a pickpocket, and the girl is his accomplice—the thief-catcher has my wallet as proof." He glared at the thief-catcher.

The thief-catcher withdrew the black leather wallet from inside his coat and casually laid it on the desk. One wallet.

Betsey frowned. "What about the other one?" she piped up. "He took two wallets out of my pocket."

The thief-catcher's eyes narrowed and for a brief second he looked as if he was going to strike her.

The stout gentleman's mouth fell open at Betsey's outburst. Then he threw back his head and guffawed loudly. "Ha, ha, ha! The girl admits she had the wallets—ha, ha! But now she wants the thief-catcher to be honest and cough up the other one! Ha, ha, ha!"

The thief-catcher reddened and quickly turned to the magistrate. "Here is the other wallet, your honor," he said, laying the second beside the first. "The gentleman asked for evidence to support his charges, so of course I submitted his wallet first. I fully intended to—"

"Yes, yes, I'm *sure* you would have," said the magistrate sarcastically. "Look, I don't have all day. Let's finish this paperwork."

While the magistrate was taking the thief-catcher's report, one of the bailiffs muttered something to Loren.

"What?" said Loren, bewildered. "What for?"

"I'm just tellin' ya, if ya got some money on ya, it's gonna go easier on you and the girl when ya get in there. Don't say I didn't warn ya."

The three men at the desk were still busy. Loren pulled Betsey aside, took the leather pouch from his waist, and shook out the coins into his hand. Counting carefully, he put half into his pocket and gave the rest to Betsey in the leather pouch.

Betsey gulped. She was sure Loren had stolen the leather pouch, too. But . . . what did it matter now? They were already caught. Her fingers closed around the pouch.

"Bailiffs!" shouted the magistrate. "Take the lad

to the men's prison, and put the girl in the women's yard. We have enough evidence to charge them both with theft—oh, wait." He turned back to Loren. "Is there someone we should inform that you and your sister have been arrested?" he asked gruffly.

Loren hung his head. "No," he said dejectedly. "No one."

❖ ❖ ❖ ❖

Once again Betsey was hustled away from Loren without a chance to say goodbye. A sullen guard escorted her through a long, cold corridor of stone, then stopped before a large wooden door reinforced with iron. Betsey could hear shrill women's voices and babies crying on the other side of the door. The guard looked briefly through a small barred window in the door before inserting the key into the lock. Without a word he swung open the door, pushed Betsey inside, then locked it behind her.

Shivering with cold and fright, Betsey stood still inside the door, trying to adjust her eyes to the dim light. Several stone steps went down in front of her into a large room in which a hundred or so women were crowded together. Several small rooms, crowded with people, jutted off the main yard on two sides. The smell was terrible, as if no one had had a bath in weeks, or the slop buckets hadn't been emptied. Probably both.

A few children, their clothes mere rags hanging on their thin bodies, gaped at the newcomer standing at the top of the steps, but everyone else ignored her. Step by step Betsey slowly descended into the room. The din sounded like a free-for-all in a street market—women arguing, babies wailing, children whining and tugging on their mothers' skirts. She cautiously made her way around bodies hunched here and there, wondering where she was supposed to sit.

"Where do ya think yer goin'?" a voice suddenly hissed at her. A short, stout woman with a round face stood menacingly in her path. Two other women joined her, glaring at Betsey.

"Can't ya see it's crowded in here?" sneered the second woman. Her head was wrapped in a dirty rag. "We don't like newcomers, see?" And the woman shoved Betsey so that she stumbled backward.

"Unless," wheedled the third woman with a mock smile, "unless you can pay the fee." This one was tall and broad-shouldered, like a man.

Betsey found her voice. "W-what fee?"

"Entrance fee," hissed the fat woman.

"For the trouble ya cause us by gettin' yerself arrested."

"So how 'bout it, girlie? Six shillings—two for each of us—and hurry up."

Betsey felt angry. She didn't want to give these dirty hags any of her money—but instinct told her she didn't have much choice. Fumbling in her pocket, she took out the leather pouch and counted out six shillings. A moment later the three bullies scurried off, laughing.

Steering clear of a prisoner who was pacing in the middle of the room talking to no one in particular, Betsey finally found a space along the wall to stand. A moment later she was startled by a raspy, hacking sound near her elbow. Squinting into a dark corner a few feet away, she saw an old woman lying on some dirty straw, wheezing and coughing and spitting on the floor.

Betsey shrank back. How long she stood against the wall, she wasn't sure, but in time the light coming in from the iron-grated opening on the far wall began to fade. Slowly she slid to the floor. Night was coming, and it was beginning to sink in that she was going to have to sleep in this hellish place. A few straw tick mattresses were scattered here and there on the floor, but each one was already occupied by one or more persons. Her stomach growled; she hadn't had anything to eat since the wonderful jelly tart Loren had bought for her that morning. *Don't they feed people in prison?* she thought angrily. At the workhouse she at least had broth and bread and potatoes.

Betsey's clothes were still damp from the early morning rain, and she shivered uncontrollably as she huddled against the stone wall. *Why* did she and Loren run away from the workhouse? This was all Loren's fault! He should have left her alone. Her muscles still ached from hauling coal at the factory—but at least at the workhouse she had something to eat, and a bed to sleep in, and there wasn't this . . . this horrible, disgusting smell that made her want to gag and throw up.

In the midst of her raging thoughts, a quiet voice in her ear startled her. "Come on, girl. You can lie down on my straw tick."

In the near darkness, Betsey could only make out a tall female figure with long, stringy hair bending

47

over her. But the voice was young and kind.

For a few moments Betsey was frozen with fear and doubt. But a hand reached out, gently pulled her to her feet, and led her to a mattress nearby. The older girl lay down—awkwardly, it seemed to Betsey—then pulled Betsey down beside her. The mattress was lumpy with old straw—but it was better than the cold stone floor.

"My name's Flori," Betsey's benefactor whispered, pulling a thin blanket over both of them.

"I'm Betsey," Betsey whispered back. Nothing more was said, but the warmth of another body soon stopped the younger girl's shivering. In spite of the coughing and rustling and stink all around her, Betsey finally slept.

Chapter 5

The Visitor

QUIT SHOVING!" screeched a woman's voice. "Touch me again and I'll kill you!"

"I was here first!" another voice yelled.

Betsey opened her eyes. Who was screaming? What was that awful smell? Where was she?

Then she remembered. She was inside Newgate Prison—and she didn't feel so good.

She raised her aching head off the mattress and looked around. The fat woman who had forced Betsey

to pay an "entrance fee" was having a kicking and shoving match with another prisoner as two guards tried to haul a big kettle down the steps. A third guard raised a stick threateningly as the fight continued. "Stop it, you shrews! Ya want to spill the stuff now? Then where would ya be?"

The two women reluctantly parted, glaring at each other. The other prisoners crowded around the kettle, each one trying to dip a bowl into the thin, runny stuff.

Betsey felt Flori stirring. "What's in the kettle?" she whispered to the older girl. Her voice sounded hoarse.

"Breakfast," Flori muttered. "It's the only meal we get in here. The rest of our food we gotta buy from the guards—or beg from visitors."

"But I don't have a bowl!"

"You can use mine today—just go get some for me first, like a good girl, will you?"

Betsey took the bowl Flori handed her and tried to find an opening around the kettle. Finally she pushed her way in like she saw the others doing, dunked the bowl, and came up with what looked like lumpy mush. Carefully she took it back to the mattress, where the other girl was sitting up now, wrapped in the blanket. In the daylight Flori looked about nineteen or twenty. Her face was thin and pale, but if her auburn hair were clean and brushed, Betsey thought, she'd be kind of pretty.

As the older girl took the bowl and swallowed the mush, Betsey realized with a start that under the ill-fitting, dirty dress Flori was wearing, her stomach was large and round. She looked like she was expecting a baby—soon.

Flori caught her staring. "What's the matter, girl? Ain't you never seen a pregnant woman before? Now go and get yourself some of that mush."

Betsey took Flori's bowl and went back to the kettle. She had just scraped some more mush off the bottom when a rough hand jerked her up by her dress.

"Seconds? Ya think yer entitled to *seconds*, eh?" a shrill voice screeched, and Betsey felt a slap on the side of her face. It was the same wild-looking, fat woman.

"Leave her alone, Bixby!" Moving swiftly for a woman in her condition, Flori pushed herself between Betsey and her tormentor. "The kid ain't had any yet; I loaned her my bowl. Now get yer hands off her."

The woman named Bixby let go of Betsey's dress and moved off, laughing strangely.

"Stay out of her way," Flori said under her breath as she navigated Betsey back to the mattress. "She's a mean one, old Bixby is. Murdered somebody with a knife."

Betsey nodded nervously, her face still stinging from the brief encounter. She tilted the bowl to her mouth. The mush tasted flat and lukewarm—but it helped ease the pinch in her stomach. When she was done, Flori took the bowl and wiped it with the edge of her dress.

Betsey studied Flori. What a terrible place for a woman who was going to have a baby! What would happen to her if the baby was born here in the prison? Who was going to help her? Curiosity finally got the best of Betsey. "Does your . . . husband know you're here?" she asked.

Flori snorted. "You mean the baby's father? *He's* the reason I'm in here," she said bitterly. "Oh, yeah, he promised we was gonna get married—when he got some money to support me and the baby, ya know. Then he got in some kind of trouble and sweet-talked me into forging a bank note for him because he can't read or write—but guess who got caught." Flori's eyes blazed. "Ain't heard from him since."

Betsey's anger flared. How unfair! But just then she was distracted by a commotion at the door to the women's yard. Again the door opened wide on its great creaking hinges, but this time a woman in a crisp white bonnet and plain gray dress stood framed in the doorway between several prison guards.

"Ya really don't want to go in there, Missus," said one of the guards bluntly. "These ain't nice ladies like yerself—bunch of witches and animals, that's what."

The woman just stood there for a moment, cradling a book in one arm, surveying the crowded room. Her face had a pained look. "Yes . . . yes, I do want to go in," she said firmly. "Please go away and leave me with the prisoners."

Betsey stared. Where had she seen this woman before? Her face and bonnet, her voice, seemed familiar somehow.

And then she remembered: She was the Quaker woman who had spoken kindly to her at the dock the

day her mother was transported!

Astonished, Betsey watched as the lady moved boldly into the filthy prison yard. Some of the prisoners stared at her openly. Her gray silk dress, with no ornaments or decorations, was elegant compared to the pitiful rags most were wearing. Others pretended to ignore her. A few, like Bixby and her cohorts, muttered angrily at this intrusion.

The visitor went directly to a sad-looking woman nursing an infant. Two other little ones hung onto her skirt. "What are their names?" Betsey heard her ask. "Oh, look at those big eyes! Why, he's just about the size of my own little boy."

The lady in gray moved from mother to mother, asking about their children, gently touching small heads here and there. To Betsey's amazement, she found *something* to admire about each scrawny, runny-nosed child.

By now all eyes were on the visitor. What was a lady like her doing in a place like this? Who was she? What did she want?

As if reading the questions in their eyes, the lady raised her voice so all could hear. "Friends, my name is Elizabeth Fry," she said clearly. "Several years ago I visited the women's prison here at Newgate— and quite frankly, my heart has not been at peace ever since. Many of you are mothers; I, too, am a mother. I am distressed for thy children. Is there not something we can do for these innocent little ones? Dost thou want them to grow up to become real prisoners themselves? Are they to learn to become thieves and worse?"

An agonized wail cut through the air as one of the mothers clutched her small child to her breast. Soon others were crying and pressing close to this Quaker woman who had touched the unspoken fear in every prison mother's heart.

"But what can we do?" a mother asked desperately.

"I have no answers," the visitor said. "But with God's help, maybe together we can do something. I would like thy permission to come visit thee regularly—woman to woman, mother to mother."

There was an astonished silence.

"*Our* permission?" someone finally said. A bitter laugh tittered around the circle of staring women.

"Get out of here!" screeched Bixby. "You do-gooder Quakers are all alike—with your 'thees' and 'thous.' Makes you feel so *Christian* to come visit the poor prisoners in Newgate, eh? But we don't need to see yer purty silk dress to remind us of what we ain't got."

"Be quiet, Bixby!" a young woman snapped. Betsey hadn't noticed this woman before, but she didn't have the hard, cold look of some of the other prisoners. "It can't hurt to talk to someone from outside—it would help remind us we're still human beings, not just trash. I say let her visit."

"Hear, hear!" Flori said. Other voices murmured in agreement.

Elizabeth Fry held up her hand. "What is thy name, friend?"

"Mary Conners." The young woman had plain features and mousy brown hair, but there was a lively look in her eye.

"I appreciate thy confidence in a stranger, dear

Mary. But Bix—er—Mrs. Bixby has a point. The silk dress was thoughtless of me. Thee won't see it again."

The visitor held out the book she was carrying. "Would the children like to hear a story Jesus told? I think everyone would like it."

The eager cries of the children and their mothers overrode the few muttered protests. In spite of her headache, Betsey felt a twinge of wonder. When was the last time she had listened to a story? Spying a stool lying on its side, she eagerly snatched it up and brought it for the visitor to sit on. Betsey sank down on the floor near the stool, trying to ignore the smell of unwashed bodies pressing close on every side as the lady began to read: "The kingdom of heaven is like a farmer who went out early in the morning to hire laborers to work in his vineyard . . ."

Soon the prison room was hushed except for the magnetic voice reading from the Bible. Some of the words were strange, but Betsey caught most of the story, which told how the farmer kept going back to the marketplace every few hours, each time hiring a few more workers. Even when the work day was almost over, the farmer found a few more idle fellows still standing around and hired *them*, too.

When the workday was over, the owner of the vineyard said to his foreman, "Call the laborers, and pay them their wages, beginning with the last one we hired and ending with the first.

When the workers who had been hired

last—about five o'clock in the afternoon—came
in from the vineyard, they were paid one coin.

Mrs. Fry stopped and explained, "This coin was a
full day's wage in those days."

"*A full day's wage!*" Flori said scornfully. "But
they'd hardly worked at all!"

"Thee is right!" the lady agreed. She seemed
pleased at the interruption. "It doesn't seem fair,
does it? But listen to what happened."

She found her place in the Bible and continued
reading.

When those who had been hired in the
morning stepped forward to be paid, they expected to receive more. But they also each
received one coin.

"What's this?" they said. "These workers
who put in only one hour received as much as
us, but we worked a full day, right through
the heat of the sun."

But the farmer answered one of them, and
said, "Friend, I've done you no wrong. You
agreed to work all day for one coin. So take
what you've earned, and be on your way. If I
want to pay these who I hired last as much as
I pay you, what's it to you? Can't I do what I
want with my own money?

So shall the last be first, and the first shall
be last.

Elizabeth Fry closed the book. The prisoners shifted uncomfortably. No one wanted to admit that she didn't understand what the story was saying.

Their visitor looked up, her eyes shining. "Don't you see, dear friends? It is never too late to come to the Savior! Thee may have wasted thy life thus far—like the men standing all day idle in the market-place. But God is like the generous landowner, offering His salvation equally to all. If thee will repent of thy wicked ways, thee, too, can have the hope of heaven."

"Easy for *you* to say," sneered Bixby. "You ain't already livin' in *hell*."

A few women laughed rudely, and the spell was broken. The crowd broke up noisily, returning to the few feet of space each had staked out for her personal belongings. Betsey got stiffly to her feet, realizing her headache had gotten worse.

"My coppers—somebody stole my coppers!" a voice suddenly screeched. Immediately accusations began flying about who stole the copper pennies while they were listening to the story. Soon more women had joined in, arguing, pushing, and taking sides.

"You better go," Mary Conner said urgently to Elizabeth Fry, gently pulling her toward the steps leading up to the prison door. Flori and Betsey tagged along, looking back nervously at the noisy brawl.

"With all due respect to you, Mrs. Fry," Mary added frankly, "it's hard to think about religion when one is living like an animal without food or decent clothes."

The Quaker woman squeezed Mary's hand, a troubled look on her kind face. A moment later the wood and iron door swung open, then was locked once more. The visitor was gone.

"I'll bet a copper that's the last we'll ever see o' *her*!" Bixby's voice cackled behind them gleefully.

Betsey winced. The pain in her head was sharper now, and Bixby's shrill voice felt like a hatpin sticking into her scalp. If only she could lie down for a little while.

Chapter 6

"A Prison Is a Prison"

THEE SAYS HER NAME IS BETSEY? How long has she been like this?" an anxious voice asked. But the voice seemed far away, floating in and out of Betsey's consciousness like a dream.

She didn't want to wake up. In her dream, she and Loren were walking hand in hand in the sunshine, eating warm jelly tarts and laughing. But then a cold rain soaked her . . . she was wet and shivering . . . and her chest hurt, as if it were on fire.

"Her clothes were damp when she came three days ago, and the next day she had a bad headache—the same day you came to visit." It was Flori's voice. "Then she got sick with a bad cough."

Jelly tarts . . . shivering cold rain . . . jelly tarts . . . fire in her chest.

"What do the prison officials do when someone gets sick like this child?"

"Do? Ha! They don't do nothin', that's what. There's supposed to be an infirmary in the jail somewhere, but no sick people have been taken there since I've been here."

The voices kept prodding Betsey into wakefulness.

"There is no effort to separate the sick from the healthy?"

"Huh! Does it look as though they separate anyone in here?" Flori said. "Sick or healthy, murderers or pickpockets, children or criminals—it's all the same to the jailers."

Jelly tarts were fading . . . just the fire in her chest.

"Betsey? Betsey, wake up, child."

Betsey opened her eyes. A stiff white bonnet framed the concerned face of Elizabeth Fry as the woman bent over her.

"Here, child, drink this broth."

Betsey struggled to sit up. The broth was warm and salty, but it hurt to swallow. She sank back on the straw mat, coughing.

The Quaker woman turned to Flori. "Thou art very kind, but not very wise, dear Flori, to share thy bed with a sick child," she chided. "Thee must take care of thyself, too—and the babe thee carries."

Flori shrugged. "Betsey and me—we keep each

other warm."

Just then Mary Conner appeared. "The clean clothes you brought have been passed out to all the women, Mrs. Fry," she said. "But . . . some of the women want to wash before putting them on." It was a plea.

"Of course! A good idea." Elizabeth Fry bustled off with Mary. The prison guards were called. Betsey could see Mrs. Fry arguing with them. But eventually a kettle of water was lugged into the yard and a fire was built. Soap was passed out.

Flori was grinning as she and Betsey watched the flurry. "That Fry woman is quite a lady," the older girl said admiringly. She turned to Betsey. "Do you know what she told me when I told her your name was Betsey? She had a little girl named Betsey, too—but she died a year ago. Five years old she was."

"Was she . . . I mean, was her Betsey her only little girl?" Betsey croaked hoarsely.

Flori chuckled. "Not likely. I think she has about nine more children."

Mrs. Fry came back to see Betsey carrying a small bundle. "I have some clothes for thee, Betsey," she said. "But I don't think thee should wash and take a chill till thou art much better." She turned to Flori. "I'm not a doctor, and can't be sure, but I've nursed a lot of illness with my ten children—nine, now"—a cloud seemed to pass over her face, then was gone—"and I think the child may have bronchitis. I'll try to get a doctor for her. In the meantime, put these clothes over the ones she's got and keep her as warm as possible. And make her drink lots of this broth. Now," she said, waving Flori away with a smile, "I'll sit with the patient, and thee can get washed and put on thy clean clothes."

Flori took the small bit of soap Mrs. Fry gave her and headed for the kettle heating over the open fire.

Just then Betsey had a coughing spasm. When it was over, she realized Elizabeth Fry was looking at her intently. "Thee looks familiar to me, child. Have we met before?"

Betsey nodded, embarrassed. "Three years ago at the dock," she whispered hoarsely. "My brother and I—we came to the dock to try to see our Mama . . . before—" Hot tears suddenly sprang to her eyes.

Mrs. Fry's eyes opened wide in recognition. "Thy mother was transported to Botany Bay?"

Betsey nodded miserably.

"And now . . . what is the charge against thee, child?"

Betsey hung her head. "S-stealing," she mumbled. "Loren and I . . . we needed money." In spite of her hoarse voice, the whole story came out.

"I see," said Mrs. Fry. There was a long silence against the background clamor of women and children washing and dressing in the clean used garments donated by Mrs. Fry's Quaker friends. Then the woman said quietly, "Have you not been taught right from wrong, child? The Good Book says, 'Thou shalt not steal.'"

Suddenly angry, Betsey rolled over, turning her back on her visitor. She couldn't bear Mrs. Fry's disapproval. What did ladies like her know about being hungry or surviving on the street anyway? Besides, what did it matter now? She might as well be in Newgate Prison. She had no other place to go.

A few minutes later, Betsey heard Mrs. Fry talking to some of the mothers. "Dear friends, ignorance is an enemy—a prison of the soul. Thee must continue to teach thy children and liberate their spirits—even while thy bodies are imprisoned behind these stone walls."

There was an awkward silence. Then one of the mothers said, "But how can we do that? Most of us ain't educated ourselves."

"I see." Another silence. Then, "Is there anyone in the women's yard who can read and write? Try to find out, and if you will choose a schoolteacher from among yourselves, I will try to obtain books and slates."

There was an immediate babble of voices as the prisoners began arguing with each other.

"What? A school here in Newgate? That's the craziest idea I've ever heard."

"No, it's not! It's exactly what the children need."

"Huh! Who could learn anything in this pit, anyway. Dirt, lice, stink—some school."

"The prison officials ain't gonna send us no schoolteacher anyway—you can bet your life on it."

"Exactly. That's why we must choose our own schoolteacher—like Mrs. Fry said."

"Ha! Ain't no schoolteacher here—in case ya hadn't noticed, most of us got caught thievin' or prostitutin'—or worse."

"Friends! Friends!" Mrs. Fry's voice rose above the rest. "Just think and talk about it. We can make plans the next time I come. But before I leave, how about another story from the Bible?"

And soon the soothing voice of Elizabeth Fry wafted toward Betsey's mattress. "A certain man had two sons: And the younger of them said, 'Father, give me my inheritance.' So the father divided wealth and gave half to his younger son. A few days later, the younger son packed his things and took a long journey into a far country. There he wasted everything he had on wild living."

❖ ❖ ❖ ❖

The next day a local doctor, accompanied by several guards, paid a visit to the women's yard in Newgate Prison. Immediately there was an uproar as women of all ages surrounded him, telling him their complaints and demanding medicine or bandages or salves.

The doctor, an old gentleman with muttonchop whiskers and sagging cheeks, looked petrified. "Get back! Go away, I say!" he said, trying to wrest his coat sleeve away from grabbing hands. "Guards, guards! Help!"

The prison guards used their sticks to beat back the unruly crowd. The doctor soon made it clear that he had come only to see two specific prisoners: an old woman with consumption, and a young girl with

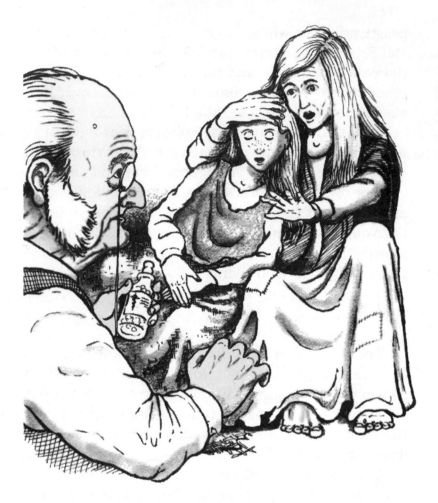

bronchitis. After examining the old woman with the raspy cough in the corner, he picked his way across the yard, looking for Betsey.

"Those meddling Quakers," the doctor muttered to himself as he looked hopelessly for a clean place to kneel beside the mound of straw where Betsey lay wrapped in three layers of clothing. "Why don't they keep their religion to themselves?" He listened to Betsey's chest. "Hmm, maybe there's hope for the girl," he mumbled, fumbling in his bag. "But medicine will only be wasted on the old woman. Bah!"

The doctor gave Betsey a big spoonful of bitter-tasting medicine, then got to his feet. "You—guards!" he said impatiently. "Get a litter and take the old woman up to the prison infirmary. The girl can walk. Come along with me, missy."

"No!" said Flori. "I'll—I'll take care of her here."

The prison doctor was about to protest, but then he shrugged. What did he care? He handed the bottle of medicine to be given three times a day to Flori, then turned on his heel, eager to get away from the foul, stinking place.

✧ ✧ ✧ ✧

After two days of medicine, Betsey was feeling much better. The cough lingered, but the headache was gone and so was the raw, burning feeling in her chest. But the broth Mrs. Fry had brought was long gone, and Betsey was hungry.

"Mrs. Ripley had visitors yesterday," Flori confided, nodding toward a prisoner with long braids wound around her head. "They brought her some food, but she might be willing to sell some if you've got a few coppers. She wants money to buy gin from the guards."

Betsey felt the pocket of her skirt underneath the other layers of clothes Mrs. Fry had brought. The leather pouch Loren had given her was still there.

"Careful!" Flori warned in a whisper as Betsey fished for the pouch. "Don't let anyone see what you're doing—or that pouch'll be gone in the middle of the night."

The loaf of bread Mrs. Ripley sold Betsey for two coppers was enough for both her and Flori to fill their stomachs for a couple of days. For a brief moment, Betsey felt badly about helping Mrs. Ripley buy gin with her coppers. She remembered Mrs. Hinkley forgetting to cook for her children while she finished off a bottle of gin in a drunken stupor. Then Betsey shrugged. She couldn't help what Mrs. Ripley did with her coppers.

Now that she was starting to feel better, Betsey was worried about Flori. Her friend looked even thinner—except for her protruding belly, which seemed larger each day. Betsey tore off another hunk of bread for Flori before wrapping the rest in Flori's blanket to save for their next meal.

A loud argument out in the corridor on the other side of the prison door caught their attention. "It sounds like Mrs. Fry!" Flori said, getting up awkwardly. Several of the other prisoners had heard the commotion too and gathered curiously near the door.

They heard the key in the lock and the prison door swung open. There stood Elizabeth Fry and the prison warden, a pudgy man who was shaped something like a turnip, accompanied as usual by several leering guards eyeing the younger women prisoners.

"It would be a waste of time!" the warden was

saying to Mrs. Fry. "A prison is a *prison*—not some fancy house for ladies down on their luck. These are criminals, for heaven's sake!"

"They are women awaiting trial—not pigs in a pigsty," Mrs. Fry protested.

"They *smell* like pigs in a pigsty!" joked one of the guards, setting off rowdy laughter among the rest.

Mrs. Fry gave the guards a withering look, then turned back to the warden. "I insist that the prison officials provide some means to clean up this women's yard. No human being should have to live in this filth."

"Sorry, lady," another guard interrupted. "It ain't *our* job to play servant maids to this scum. Our job is just to keep 'em under lock and key so they can't kill or rob anybody else."

The warden shrugged. "See? There's no one to do the job. Now if I were you, Mrs. Fry, I wouldn't bother—"

"So! No one willing to do the job? Is that the issue?" The Quaker woman's eyes were flashing. She turned and faced the restless female prisoners who had gathered to witness the strange argument. "Dear friends," she said, raising her voice so all could hear, "the good warden is willing to provide cleaning supplies—soap, water, scrub brushes, and barrels for trash. Are you willing to do the work to clean up your own surroundings? If not for yourselves, for your innocent children?"

The warden's mouth gaped open. "I'm willing to supply—*what*?"

Chapter 7

Newgate School

FLORI WAS THE FIRST TO SPEAK UP. "I'll do it! I don't want my baby born in this squalor."

"That's right! The children are getting sick."

"We need shovels!"

"And fresh straw!"

"Water!"

"Soap!"

The noisy, demanding din in the women's prison yard rose and continued until, several hours later, a reluctant warden supervised the delivery of trash barrels, shovels, fresh straw, soap, water, and scrub brushes. The prisoners started grabbing for brushes and soap, accompanied by kicks and hair pulling if two women laid a hand on the same brush.

"Animals!" said the warden in disgust. "Mark my words, Mrs. Fry, nothing's going to help this lot."

"Just leave us. We'll sort it out ourselves," said Mrs. Fry firmly. As the warden left and the great iron door swung shut, the Quaker woman spoke loudly but calmly as she moved into the scuffle, "Friends! Friends! May I have your attention please?"

Gradually the bickering and fighting quieted, and the prisoners gathered around Elizabeth Fry. "The first thing you must do," she said, "is choose several leaders from among yourselves and organize yourselves into work teams—nine or ten would do. Then the work can be divided up and supplies distributed."

The prisoners just stared at her, confused.

"Why don't you just choose the leaders?" said Kitty Blunt, Bixby's tall, broad-shouldered friend. She had a challenging look in her eye.

"No," said Elizabeth Fry firmly, "you must choose your own leaders. This is your prison yard, and you should have a say in how you want things done." With that, Mrs. Fry took a stool to a corner of the room and sat down.

The prisoners looked at one another in confusion. But first one person and then another suggested one of their fellow prisoners to be a leader. When a suggestion was seconded with several assenting voices, then it was decided. Soon ten leaders had been picked, including Bixby and Mary Conner.

"Good," said Mrs. Fry. "Now you leaders divide up the work and choose your work teams."

The organizing process took a little while, with much shouting and arguing, but finally small groups of women were shoveling up old straw and dirt into the barrels, emptying slop buckets into the trench that ran outside and sloshing clean water after the waste, scrubbing the floor, and distributing clean straw for bedding, while one team took care of the youngest children.

Mary Conner chose Flori and Betsey to be on her team, but they were scrubbing part of the prison floor and Flori didn't want Betsey's cough to get worse by getting wet. So Betsey helped the team that distributed fresh, sweet-smelling straw to every person or family group. But even that effort set her to coughing.

When the work was done, the prisoners looked both exhausted and proud of the change they'd produced in their surroundings. There was also a distinct difference in the way the women were relating to one another. Maybe they were just tired, or maybe it was the effect of working together, but for the first time since Betsey had come to Newgate, no one was fighting or arguing or slapping someone else.

"Excellent," Mrs. Fry said, looking around approvingly. "The children have a clean 'home,' and they can concentrate on something else besides dirt and bugs. Now . . . have you chosen a schoolteacher yet?"

The prisoners looked at each other. Had this Quaker lady actually been serious about starting their own *school?*

"Why not?" Flori spoke up boldly. "We chose our own leaders just now to clean up this place. Why can't we choose a schoolteacher?" The pregnant girl looked around boldly. "I nominate Mary Conners. She's had book learnin', an all she done wrong was steal her pappy's watch back after her brother pawned it. She don't pick fights, either—not like some people I could name."

Flori glared at Bixby and her friends. Kitty Blunt—the tall one—snorted, and Bixby and Sally Webb just shrugged indifferently.

There was an immediate buzz among the rest of the prisoners, with general head nodding.

"We agree," several spoke up.

"Mary?" Mrs. Fry said. "Are you willing to undertake this task?"

For a brief moment Mary Conner seemed flustered; then she tilted her chin and looked Elizabeth Fry in the eye. "I can try," she said. "But we need a quiet room—a place the children can study and not be distracted. And books."

Mrs. Fry grinned broadly. "I'll talk to the prison warden about the room. Right now, how about a Bible story? We could all use a break."

The children cheered and gathered eagerly around Elizabeth Fry as she settled on the stool with her Bible. But Betsey noticed that all the women—even Bixby—settled somewhere nearby where they could listen to the words from Scripture.

The parable of the woman who lost a silver coin and swept and swept her house until she found it was interrupted by the warden coming into the prison yard. The man stared in astonishment, first at the greatly improved yard, and then at the quiet group of women and children listening to the Scripture. His mouth opened and closed a few times, then finally he shook his head as if trying to remember why he had come.

"Ahem! Uh . . . oh, yes, will the following prisoners step up and get their trial dates?"

Immediately the mood of the women tensed. There was an anxious silence as the warden began reading names: "Polly Bixby . . . Helen Ripley . . . Flori Alexander . . ."

About five or six more names were read. As each woman approached the warden, she was handed a piece of paper. Not many of the women could read, but they silently handed their slips to Elizabeth Fry, who quietly read each one aloud.

"When, Flori?" Betsey asked anxiously when her friend sank down on the straw, clutching the piece of paper.

"A week from Friday." The older girl bit her lip and stared silently at the floor for a while. Then she whispered, "Oh, Betsey, I'm scared. What's going to happen to me . . . and my baby?"

✧ ✧ ✧ ✧

Mrs. Fry didn't come for several days over the weekend, and the mood in the prison yard grew restless and cranky once again in spite of the cleaner quarters and the talk of starting a school. The warden's list of women facing trials the next week cast a gloom over the entire yard, and the guards did a brisk business selling gin from the prison tap as many of the prisoners tried to numb their fears.

If fat-faced Polly Bixby was worried about her trial for murder, however, she didn't show it. She and her two cronies got drunk and stayed drunk for three days straight. They laughed loudly and played cards and bullied anyone who got in their way. Sometimes one of the braver women refused to be bullied, which usually ended in a noisy fight.

Flori, however, was depressed, and just sat on the mattress not talking to Betsey. Even though Betsey's name hadn't come up for trial yet, Flori's mood affected the younger girl, and she too brooded about what was going to happen to her—and Loren.

Was her brother all right? Loren was right here in Newgate—but he might as well be on the moon. Betsey didn't know what was happening to him, or even if she'd ever see him again! Did he know she'd been sick? Was he getting enough to eat? Had anyone befriended him, or was he all alone in the men's prison yard? What would his punishment be?

Flori and Betsey's dejected silence was broken only by an occasional raspy cough from Betsey. Finally, hunger broke the spell; they ate the last of their bread and tried to figure out how to get more food. Betsey noticed that some of the prisoners begged from passersby through the grated window at one end of the yard. She and Flori decided to take turns begging, and whoever got money or food would share with the other one.

When the prison door swung open on Monday afternoon and Elizabeth Fry entered the yard, Betsey welcomed the visit with great relief. Maybe Mrs. Fry could find out how Loren was doing for her!

But before Betsey had time to ask her favor, Mrs. Fry announced matter-of-factly that she had met that morning with the prison officials who insisted that there was no room in the jail available for such a school. "I asked if that was their only objection," said Mrs. Fry, "and they said, yes, that was the problem. So . . . what do you women say?" She looked around at the sea of faces around her, a slight smile on her lips. "Can we find a solution to the room problem?"

The women immediately began talking all at once. Some were angry because the prison officials were stalling; others were upset because maybe the school wouldn't happen after all.

"What about using one of our own rooms off the yard?" Betsey spoke up. The rooms were little more than large, unlocked cells that some of the women—mostly mothers with children—used to give them a little more privacy.

"The kid's got a point," someone said. "They've already given those rooms to us to use. We wouldn't even have to ask."

"But those rooms are not that big!" protested

76

Helen Ripley. "Will there be enough room for all the children?"

"It will do for a start," Mary Conner spoke up. "I counted all the children of prisoners between the ages of five and thirteen, plus the youngest prisoners like Betsey Maxwell—and that comes to thirty children. We can manage."

Betsey's heart leaped. She was going to be allowed to go to the school? Whenever Elizabeth Fry had talked about the plight of the "innocent children" locked up with their mothers in Newgate Prison, she had never included herself. She wasn't "innocent"—the thief-catcher would testify to that.

There was some grumbling by the women who were occupying the side room chosen for the school, but the other women helped them get settled among the other rooms and out in the yard. As Elizabeth Fry was getting ready to leave, Betsey remembered the favor she wanted to ask.

"I don't know, Betsey," the Quaker woman said kindly. "I've been given permission to visit the women's yard, but the men's yards are off limits to women visitors other than family. But . . . I'll see what I can do."

❖ ❖ ❖ ❖

The next day when Elizabeth Fry came to visit, she was not alone. Two other women dressed in the plain dress of the Quakers were with her, and all three women were carrying bulging sacks. As the contents of the sacks were emptied, the children gasped in delight: reading books, slates, and chalk! Mary Conner was given a record book, an ink bottle, and a pen to write the name of each child and to keep

a record of his or her progress.

Mothers and other curious women crowded in the doorway to watch the first lesson: to draw the letter *A* on the slates. Betsey shared a slate with one of Helen Ripley's children, a seven-year-old named Sissy. At first she felt awkward being just as ignorant as someone half her age, but as they sounded out and drew new letters each day, Betsey was quickly absorbed in the excitement of learning. Soon she would know how to read!

But on Thursday Sissy didn't come to the "schoolroom," and Betsey had the slate to herself. When Mary Conner dismissed the children for the day, Betsey looked around the yard and saw Mrs. Ripley slumped in a corner hugging a bottle of gin. Sissy and her two little brothers hung anxiously on Flori's skirts as she tried to comfort them.

"What's the matter?" Betsey asked Flori.

Flori's jaw tightened. "She had her trial today. Guilty of theft. Sentenced to transportation."

Betsey swallowed. "When?"

Flori shrugged. "Whenever the ships come in from Botany Bay."

Betsey looked around the yard. In all her excitement at getting to attend the little prison school, she had almost forgotten the trials. "Where's old Binby?" she wondered.

"Gone. Sentenced to hang for the murder of her husband. They took her to wait in the execution cells."

Betsey's mouth went dry. The stupid judges

should have transported Bixby, not Mrs. Ripley, she thought—and good riddance. But *hanging*? It was too terrible to think of, even for Bixby.

Friday was Flori's trial for forgery. Elizabeth Fry went with her to plead mercy for the youthful mother-to-be. Betsey couldn't concentrate on her letters and finally asked Mary Conner if she could be excused from lessons. Sympathetically, Mary nodded. Worried, Betsey waited near the door to the yard as one hour, then two, dragged by.

Finally she heard footsteps in the corridor outside. The door was unlocked and Elizabeth Fry and Flori came down the steps. Tight-lipped and strained, Mrs. Fry gently helped Flori to her mattress, where the girl covered her face with her hands.

Betsey anxiously searched Mrs. Fry's face.

"Guilty," said the older woman sadly. "The judge called it a 'grievous felony against the Bank of England.'"

"And the sentence?" Betsey's heart was pounding.

"Transportation to Botany Bay for seven years—after the baby is born."

At first, relief washed over Betsey. She'd heard that some people were hung for forgery. Then she had another terrible realization: if Flori were exiled to Botany Bay, Betsey would lose the only friend she had in prison—in fact, the *only* friend she had!

Chapter 8

The Plot

BETSEY. BETSEY MAXWELL!"

Betsey's head jerked up. She'd been staring at her slate in the tiny prison schoolroom without really seeing the letters that little Sissy Ripley had written there.

"Betsey!" Mary Conner raised her voice, trying to be heard over the restless chatter of spectators in the narrow doorway. In the background, noisy arguments could also be heard from the main yard. "Can you recite the three letters Sissy wrote on your slate?"

Squinting her eyes in the dim light, Betsey recognized the first one—*B*—and the last one—*D*. But what was that middle letter with three legs sticking out sideways?

"*E*," whispered Sissy.

"Sound them out together," encouraged Mary. "*B* . . . *E* . . . *D* spells what word?"

Betsey just stared at the slate, her face turning red. She felt stupid, but her mind wasn't on her lessons this morning. All she'd been able to think about was Flori being exiled from England. Flori was the closest thing to family she had right now. How could she bear prison without Flori?

"Ladies!" she heard Mary Conner say to the women in the doorway. "You must be quiet. Otherwise the children can't learn."

"But we wanna learn how to read, too!" complained one of the curious young mothers, a toddler on her hip.

"You! What about us!" demanded a brash girl in her midteens, elbowing others out of her way. "How come Betsey Maxwell gets to be in the school, but we can't, huh? She's a common thief, just like the rest of us."

Instead of quieting down, the commotion in the prison yard outside grew louder. "It's Mrs. Fry and her Quaker friends!" someone cried. "And they've got food!"

Mary Conner rolled her eyes and gave up. "Class dismissed for today," she said. Immediately the children jumped up, slates clattering to the stone floor, and eagerly scrambled out of the small schoolroom.

Betsey hung back and helped Mary Conner collect the spilled slates and chalk. She wanted to talk to Elizabeth Fry and see if she'd been able to find out any news about Loren. But she knew it was useless to try and talk to her alone at the beginning of her visit when the prisoners and children crowded around, all talking at once.

"Miss Conner," she said suddenly—Mrs. Fry had instructed the children to address their teacher respectfully—"what kind of punishment do they give pickpockets?"

The prison teacher didn't answer at first, just stacked the slates carefully in a corner of the room. Then she said cautiously, "It depends. Stealing is a felony and can receive capital punishment, but—"

"What's 'capital punishment'?" Betsey frowned.

Mary Conner looked distressed. "Well . . . I-I—"

"Capital punishment," another voice interrupted, "is death by hanging. However, if the judge is merciful, a thief can be sentenced to transportation instead." Elizabeth Fry entered the little schoolroom and looked gravely at Betsey as if to emphasize the seriousness of crime. "But thee must not worry, Betsey," she added kindly. "Sometimes the judges take into consideration the age of the criminal, or a first-time offense. The important thing is to reform thy ways and make thy peace with God no matter what happens."

The pleasant-faced woman in her starched white bonnet then turned to Mary Conner. "Now, Mary, I apologize for interrupting the school. It was thoughtless of me to arrive in the middle of thy lessons."

Mary Conner smiled wryly. "They were pretty well disrupted before you arrived, Mrs. Fry. The women are so bored! They have nothing to do, so they squabble and fight. But they're all eager to learn—even the older prisoners. I wish we could teach them all," she said wistfully. "Or at least give them something to do."

A light went on in Mrs. Fry's eyes. "Something to do . . . thee is right, Mary! If they could learn useful skills, it would give them dignity *and* help them earn a living when they get out of prison. Otherwise, I fear most will end up back in Newgate Prison with even worse consequences. But thee has given me an idea. Come, let's talk to my friends and see what can be done. Coming, Betsey?"

Betsey hesitated.

"Art thou feeling ill, Betsey?" Elizabeth Fry asked.

"No, ma'am. Just a cough sometimes. But . . . is there any news about my brother?" she asked anxiously.

Mrs. Fry shook her head. "Not really. I asked the warden. All he would tell me is that Loren Maxwell is well and still awaiting trial." Mrs. Fry smiled sympathetically. "Thee mustn't worry about thy brother, Betsey; it does him no good. But thee *can* pray for him—that will do him a world of good! Now, come along, we have brought fresh bread and dried apples. Thee must have a share!"

Still Betsey didn't move. "If he is guilty, will they send him to Botany Bay?" she asked stubbornly.

Mrs. Fry sighed. "It is likely, yes."

To Mrs. Fry's surprise, Betsey smiled—a strange, distant smile—and walked out of the schoolroom.

❖ ❖ ❖ ❖

That night Betsey lay awake on the straw mat, thinking. Her mother had been put on a ship going somewhere to a place called Botany Bay, Flori had been sentenced to transportation to Botany Bay— Loren would probably get sentenced to exile in Botany Bay, too.

Botany Bay had always had a ring of terror for the women in the prison yard. It was the gateway to a wild, mysterious place some English explorer had named "New South Wales," far, far away from everything and everyone they knew and held dear. Rumors from the returning ships said there were no cities, no civilization . . . only a hot, dry, barren country with strange animals and savage people. Prisoners imagined getting dumped off the ship and left to starve or be killed by wild animals or speared by natives.

But as she stared into the darkness of Newgate Prison, trying hard not to cough and wake up Flori, all Betsey could think about was that all the people she loved best in the whole world were going to Botany Bay. And suddenly the thought of getting sentenced to "transportation" for pickpocketing lost its terror.

Next to her, Flori's shoulders shook slightly, and

Betsey realized her friend was crying silently. Betsey raised up on one elbow and patted Flori's arm.

"Don't cry, Flori," she whispered. "Everything's going to be all right. Why, we're all going to Botany Bay together!"

Flori rolled over on her back. It was so dark in the prison that the two friends could not see each other's faces, even twelve inches apart. "Wha-what do you mean?" the older girl sniffed.

"Well, I've been thinking," Betsey whispered. "They're not going to send you to Botany Bay until after your baby is born. By then my brother and I might be called up for our trial. And Mrs. Fry said it's likely that the sentence for pickpocketing will be transportation—you know, to Botany Bay, just like you!"

Flori sat up. "Do you really think—?"

The two girls sat side by side in the dark, each lost in her own thoughts. Finally Flori whispered, "Oh, Betsey, if that were true, it might be bearable. But I'm not sure they will sentence you to transportation."

It was Betsey's turn to be startled. "Why? What do you mean?"

"Because you didn't even know Loren was going to steal those wallets—you told me so yourself! *He* was the one who broke the law by picking pockets.

"But they arrested me, too. I'm in prison, aren't I?"

Flori snorted in the darkness. "Huh. You're in prison because they caught you with the wallets. That makes you an accomplice—but an 'innocent accomplice,' if you ask me. When the judge hears your case, he may decide to just send you back to the workhouse or somethin'. I mean, it's not as if you really committed a crime. And you're just a kid, for heaven's sake."

Betsey felt a new kind of terror at the thought of being sent back to the workhouse—without Loren, without Flori, and without hope of ever seeing them again.

Flori finally lay back down and fell into a fitful sleep. But the night stretched endlessly for Betsey as she pondered Flori's words. By the time the gray light of morning filtered into the women's yard at Newgate Prison, Betsey had a new resolve: if it wasn't certain that she would get transported with Flori and Loren, then she should commit another crime, one that would *guarantee* she'd get exiled to Botany Bay.

✧ ✧ ✧ ✧

Betsey's mood changed. She was quiet, watchful, always on the lookout for something she could steal that would *matter*. She thought about stealing from some of the other prisoners—things were always "going missing" in the women's yard—but quickly gave up that idea, realizing the prison officials didn't care.

Her second idea was to steal from some of the ladies who had started coming with Elizabeth Fry to visit the prison. The ladies brought extra food and good, used clothing; helped the children with their lessons; even got down on their hands and knees and helped scrub when it was time for the weekly "cleaning day." The trouble was, most of them were Quakers like Mrs. Fry, so their dresses, wraps, and bonnets were plain, with no furs or feathers or jewelry to tempt a would-be thief.

One day Elizabeth Fry gathered the women prisoners together. She had good news! The ladies who had been visiting the prison with her had formed the Ladies Newgate Committee with the specific purpose of raising money, providing materials, and helping the prisoners learn practical skills such as sewing, knitting, and "fancywork" that they could sell to help support themselves while in prison.

"I do not need to tell you that the warden and other prison officials are skeptical," she warned. "In fact, they think we are crazy!"

The prisoners snickered, but Mrs. Fry did not smile.

"They are convinced common criminals do not have the discipline to work and that the materials we provide will simply be stolen or vandalized." She looked around at the group of women, young and old, pressed around her. "*I* think they are wrong. But . . . it is up to you."

As always, the idea of being responsible for something seemed to confuse the prisoners. They shuffled restlessly, but waited for Elizabeth Fry to go on.

"For this idea to work, you must organize yourselves—just as you do for cleaning day, except more so," Mrs. Fry told the prisoners. "You will need rules, written by yourselves and agreed to by everyone. Then you must divide yourselves into work teams and appoint monitors to oversee and record the work for each team. Finally, if you will appoint a matron of the prison yard to enforce the rules—a woman whom you respect, chosen from among yourselves— then I will ask the warden that the male guards no longer enter the prison yard."

Cheers immediately erupted. The women were tired of the guards' leering looks, rude comments, and rough treatment.

Excited by the possibility of having something to do to help pass the long, boring days, weeks, and months as each waited for her trial—and earning their own money to boot—the women eagerly set to work suggesting rules, dividing into work teams, and naming candidates for work monitors and a prison matron.

In the meantime, Mrs. Fry made a point to check on Flori and Betsey during her visits. She was concerned because even though Betsey wasn't really sick, the nagging cough lingered, and the girl seemed thin and pale. Also it was nearing time for Flori to deliver her baby. Mrs. Fry was distressed that the older girl had no better place than a straw mattress in a common prison room for her "lying in." "It's barbaric!" she fumed. She even asked the warden for permission to move Flori to her own home until after the baby was born, but the warden wouldn't hear of it.

"This is a convicted *criminal*, Mrs. Fry," he snapped when the persistent woman had dragged him into the prison yard to see Flori's condition for himself. "Do you think this is the first pregnant prisoner Newgate has seen? And it won't be the last. What would happen if we let them all out to give birth? Ha! The prison birthrate would soar!"

As the warden stomped out of the women's yard, Elizabeth Fry's shoulders sagged. Betsey knew she thought the visit had ended in failure.

But for Betsey, the warden's visit was a success. As he stood arguing with Mrs. Fry, Betsey noticed a bright gold watch chain in the man's waistcoat . . . and that's when she got The Idea.

She would steal the warden's watch! *That* would surely get her convicted and guarantee that she'd be sentenced to transportation and exile to Botany Bay.

Chapter 9

The Watch

BECAUSE FLORI COULD READ AND WRITE, she was appointed to be a monitor for one of the work teams.

"It's so exciting, Betsey!" she said as the two girls shared their supper of potatoes—a gift from a Friends "Meeting" (as Quaker churches were called)—boiled in a common pot in the middle of the yard for everyone. "Today the Quaker ladies taught us how to sew patchwork quilts—and Mrs. Fry said a businessman in London is willing to buy them to sell in his store!"

The older girl blew on a hot potato. " 'Course, I'm just learning—but Mrs. Fry said I could do a small one first for

practice and keep it for my baby." Flori's face suddenly clouded. "My baby *is* going to be all right, isn't it, Betsey? I mean, traveling by ship so many months on the sea . . . ." Her lip trembled.

Betsey gave her friend a hug. "Don't worry, Flori. I will help you. We're going together, remember?"

Flori shook her head. "Stop it, Betsey! It's no use pretending. That kind of dreaming will only make it worse for both of us."

"I'm not pretending," Betsey insisted. "You'll see."

Flori looked at her sharply. "What do you mean?"

Betsey thought about telling Flori her plan, but instead busied herself with her bowl of potatoes.

"Betsey Maxwell!" Flori hissed. "Don't you dare get yourself in trouble! A second offense could get you hanged!"

"Pooh! You don't know what you're talking about!" Betsey said, standing up angrily. She shouldn't have said anything; Flori was too nervous and fearful these days.

"Don't be mad," Flori relented. "Come on, sit down and tell me what you learned in school today. Are you doing sums?"

"Yeah." Betsey sat, relieved at the change in subject. "I know two plus two equals four, three plus three equals six, four plus four equals eight— "

Flori grinned wryly. "Maybe you'll have to help me. I'm supposed to keep records of all the sewing we do, how much we get paid for the lot, then how much to pay each woman, depending on how many pieces she did! Can you believe all that figuring?"

✧ ✧ ✧ ✧

Under pressure from Elizabeth Fry and the Ladies Newgate Committee, the prison laundry was turned over to the women prisoners for a workroom. The women themselves whitewashed the walls to improve the light for sewing, while the warden was left wondering when, exactly, had he promised to provide paint and brushes if the prisoners did the work?

A routine was established that gave order to each day. Each morning Elizabeth Fry read a passage from Scripture to the children, prisoners, and visitors in her rich, calm voice. The daily stream of visitors were touched to see the prisoners respond, often with tears, to Bible passages describing the suffering Jesus went through to save people from sin. Then Mrs. Fry led the women and children in a prayer that she said had been her mainstay for many years:

"Whate'er I do in any thing,
To do it as to Thee."

The children then studied their lessons with Mary Conner, while the work teams, each under the supervision of their monitors, knitted stockings and caps, sewed patchwork, and braided rag rugs. Sometimes the members of the Ladies Newgate Committee read classic literature to the women as a way to improve their minds while they worked.

A matron had been appointed, a former housekeeper for a duke who had been accused (*wrongfully*, she insisted) of stealing from her employer. She was a no-nonsense sort of woman, but fair. Her job was to search new prisoners for knives or other dangerous items, prevent prison bullies from collecting an entrance fee from new prisoners, enforce the rules, listen to complaints, inspect the yard and various rooms after cleaning day, and accompany prisoners when they had to leave the yard. Visitors had to check in with the matron before being admitted to the yard. Even the warden stated his business with the matron first, who then summoned the prisoner in question, or accompanied the warden and his guests on their inspections.

At the end of the day, Elizabeth Fry again read a passage from Scripture before bidding the prisoners and children goodbye.

She was reading one evening when the prison warden appeared and spoke to the matron. When the Bible was closed, the matron called for attention. "The warden has a list of new trials which have been set. Will each name that is read please come receive your summons?"

As always when the warden visited the women's yard, Betsey was alert, watching for the right moment to steal the warden's watch. But this evening he was standing on the steps leading down into the women's yard, reading out the names on his list, and handing each summons to the matron who then handed it to the prisoner. Betsey didn't see any way she could get close to the warden. She'd have to wait until he came down into the yard . . . but what if he didn't? Maybe she ought to create a disturbance or—

"He called your name, Betsey!" Flori said, poking her in the side. "Go on. It's your trial date."

Betsey had been so busy plotting, she hadn't heard her name called. For a moment she felt panic; had she waited too long? She forced herself to walk up to the matron, get her paper, and bring it back to Flori.

"When?" she asked, showing Flori the paper.

"Next week . . . Thursday."

Thursday. Almost a week. But she couldn't wait for the "right" time. She had to make it happen.

✧ ✧ ✧ ✧

Flori watched as Betsey walked over to their mattress, clutching the slip of paper. The younger girl had a strange, determined look on her face.

Worried, Flori looked around for Elizabeth Fry. The Quaker woman and the other visitors were speaking to and encouraging the women who had just received their trial dates.

"Mrs. Fry? Mrs. Fry!" Flori said, moving awkwardly toward the Quaker woman as the visitors prepared to leave the women's yard.

"Flori!" said Elizabeth Fry. "Art thou all right? Is it thy time?"

"No, no, it's not the baby, Mrs. Fry. It's Betsey. I'm worried about her."

Mrs. Fry looked over to where Betsey was sitting on the mattress, coughing into her skirt. "Of course. I'll speak to her before I leave. It's always a shock to get one's trial date."

"No! You don't understand!" Flori said. "She *wants* to get sentenced. She wants to be transported with me and . . . and her brother. She keeps talking about all going together."

"Ah. I see. Don't worry, Flori. That's not likely," Mrs. Fry said reassuringly. "At worst the judge may put her in the stocks for half a day to teach her a lesson—but no doubt Loren will testify that Betsey didn't know anything about his plan to be a pickpocket. Which is a good thing," she added, "because I don't think Betsey is well enough to survive an eight-month trip on the open sea. That cough of hers worries me."

"I tried to tell her that!" Flori said, close to tears. "God knows, I wish she *would* get sentenced to transportation. It would be a great comfort to me. But—oh, Mrs. Fry, I'm afraid!"

Elizabeth Fry looked puzzled. "I don't understand, Flori. Art thou afraid of what will happen to Betsey when she is released from prison? If so, I share thy concern. She's so young, and has no family except Loren. In fact, the Ladies Newgate Committee and I have been talking about what we can do for young prisoners who get put back on the street—"

Elizabeth Fry stopped at the stricken look on Flori's face. "Flori? What is it? What makes thee afraid?"

"I-I'm afraid she's going to do something to make sure she gets sentenced to transportation—except, except—"

"What do you mean, *do something*?"

97

"I don't know! Get into trouble somehow. She's been acting very strangely. Oh, Mrs. Fry, we have to stop her! She doesn't know the risk she takes!" Flori's voice faded to a whisper. "I once saw a child swing on the gallows at Tyburn Square."

Elizabeth Fry's face went white. "I see . . . yes, I see now. Thee was right to tell me, Flori. We must both watch Betsey closely." She gently brushed Flori's tear-stained cheek. "Together with God, we must care for our young friend."

✧ ✧ ✧ ✧

"Miss Conner," Betsey said as the children jostled into the prison schoolroom the next morning, "why don't we invite the warden to come and hear us recite our lessons—as a thank-you for letting us start our school."

"Why, Betsey," Mary Conner said, "that's an excellent idea. All of you children have learned so much in the last few weeks. We could recite the alphabet, write the words you have learned, do a few sums . . ."

In no time at all, it seemed, the idea had gone from Mary Conner to the matron to Elizabeth Fry, who invited the warden personally to come to the women's yard the following Wednesday to hear the prison children recite their lessons.

The children worked hard to recite their numbers and letters with no mistakes. Several of the older students practiced reading aloud in the "readers" donated by the Ladies Newgate Committee. Somewhere between Friday and Wednesday, the mothers and other prisoners were invited to come hear their children recite, and the event was moved out of the schoolroom into the women's yard.

Flori patiently heard Betsey recite each evening as the younger girl practiced for her part. Maybe she'd been worrying about Betsey for nothing, she thought. All her young friend seemed interested in was doing a good job for the Newgate School Exhibition, as it was now being called. Rumor had it that the warden was quite pleased, and had invited several other officials and their wives to be his guests at the exhibition.

"Can I have that last piece of bread?" Betsey asked Flori on Tuesday evening as they ate their supper of bread and hard cheese—another treat from one of the Quaker "Meetings."

Flori snorted. "Every night you've been asking for the last bit of food. What are you doing—feeding a mouse in the schoolroom?"

Betsey turned red. "It's just a bitty thing. He's a prisoner, just like us."

"Huh." Flori shivered. "I hate mice—rats and bugs, too, for that matter. I've seen enough in this place to last me a lifetime. But . . . oh, well. Take it. Guess it can't hurt anything."

Wednesday arrived with great excitement. The women's yard had been scrubbed extra clean; the children had been bathed and given clean clothes. Stools and chairs mysteriously appeared for the warden and his guests to sit on. All the work teams had been given the time off to hear the children recite.

. Mary Conner was flushed and smiling. Proudly she called the whole school to stand in front of the "audience" and recite the alphabet, which they did letter perfect. Then the littlest children wrote on their slates as Miss Conner called out specific letters, and the slates were held up so all could see.

The warden's guests were quite impressed, and the warden himself was beaming. "Yes, madam," he was heard commenting to a lady guest in fancy dress, "I knew all along that the children of these prisoners just needed some expert guidance to bring out their potential."

Finally the oldest children were called upon to read a simple poem from their readers. Reading perfectly, Betsey held her reader with one hand and eased her other hand into the deep pocket of her skirt. As the guests and prisoners clapped, the boys bowed and the girls curtsyed as Miss Conner had taught them. Just at that moment, Betsey brought her hand out of her pocket and released the mouse.

"Eeeeek!" she screeched. "A mouse!"

Both the prisoners and the children had seen plenty of mice in the women's yard—but a rodent running among their feet was not something the genteel lady guests of the warden were used to. In a moment there was bedlam with ladies screaming, brave boys darting around trying to catch the mouse, and little girls jumping up and down in excitement.

In the midst of all the commotion, Betsey Max-

well moved into position next to the warden and slid
the watch out of his watch pocket, jerked the chain
free, and slipped it into the pocket of her skirt.

Chapter 10

The Promise

MARY CONNER, ELIZABETH FRY, and the matron quickly helped restore order, collecting the children and reassuring the guests. The warden looked angry, but after a few calming words from Mrs. Fry, he began to relax and smile once more. "Heh, heh, no harm done," he said to his guests. "The children recited well, didn't they? Now what's this?"

Unknown to Mrs. Fry, the work teams had asked the matron if they could display their recent handiwork from the prison workroom as a surprise. As the colorful quilts, braided rugs, and knit stockings and caps were paraded for the guests, there were *oohs* and *ahhs* from gentlemen and ladies alike.

Betsey was glad for the further distraction. Her heart was beating fast; she needed a moment to think. What was going to happen next? At some point the warden would miss his watch, there would be a search, and she would be discovered—

"Betsey?" It was Elizabeth Fry, whispering in her ear. "Come with me." Warily Betsey followed the Quaker woman into the empty schoolroom.

"Give me what is in thy pocket, Betsey," Mrs. Fry said gravely.

Betsey opened her mouth to protest, then realized maybe it didn't matter. She'd been caught with the watch; no question *this* time that it was her own doing. In fact, maybe it was better this way. Mrs. Fry would protect her from the angry warden until it was time for her trial, when she would be found guilty and sentenced to transportation to Botany Bay.

She shrugged and handed over the watch. Without a word Mrs. Fry left the schoolroom and returned to the activity in the women's yard, smiling and visiting with the prisoners and guests. Watching from the doorway of the schoolroom, Betsey was confused; why didn't Mrs. Fry speak to the warden and admit who'd taken his watch?

Finally, as the warden was preparing to leave with his guests, Elizabeth Fry called out to him, "Warden! Wait one moment." She hurried over, smiling pleasantly. "I believe this may be yours?" And she held out the watch.

Startled, the warden quickly felt his empty watch pocket, and his face darkened. "*What—?*" he thundered, snatching the watch and chain out of Mrs. Fry's hand. "Who stole my—?"

"Oh, my!" Mrs. Fry said with a wave of her hand and a little laugh. "There was so much excitment during the mouse episode . . . so confusing. But thy watch is found now, and all is well."

Betsey was confused. What was happening? Why didn't Mrs. Fry tell the warden that she, Betsey Maxwell, had *stolen* the watch? She saw the warden stuff the watch back into his watch pocket, muttering angrily to himself; Elizabeth Fry turned away, as if there was nothing more to be said. All of a sudden, Betsey realized her chance to commit another crime and be transported to Botany Bay was disappearing.

Gathering her courage, Betsey boldly walked over to the steps leading out of the women's yard. *I stole it!* she would say. *Me! Betsey Maxwell!*

But just as she opened her mouth to speak out, the warden suddenly turned back and shouted, "Mrs. Fry!"

Betsey was so startled, she stopped short. Elizabeth Fry—and everyone else, for that matter—turned toward the warden.

"Mrs. Fry! If I find out that one of these *urchins* stole my watch," he blustered, red-faced, shaking his finger at the Quaker woman, "I'll see to it that she swings from Tyburn gallows! Stealing property from a government official is a crime punishable by death. You mark my words!"

With that the warden turned on his heel and took his portly frame out the prison door.

Betsey suddenly felt faint, as if all the blood was draining out of her head. *The gallows!* Flori was right! And she'd almost—

She glanced quickly at Elizabeth Fry, but her Quaker friend looked away, as if not wanting to call attention to Betsey. Shakily, Betsey stumbled over to the mattress she shared with Flori and sank down onto the straw mat.

Mrs. Fry had literally saved her neck.

She didn't look at Flori. Flori could almost read her soul and would know it was she who had stolen the warden's watch. Flori didn't say anything, but simply put an arm around Betsey and pulled her close.

It was too much for Betsey. "Oh, Flori," she broke down, sobs shaking her body, "what am I going to do now? My trial is tomorrow. What's going to happen? I want to be transported with you! I've got to! I can't stay here alone—without you, without Loren! What if . . . what if—"

"Hush," Flori said, holding Betsey and rocking her like her mother used to. "Hush."

❖ ❖ ❖ ❖

That night Betsey awoke to hear Flori moaning and panting beside her on the straw mat.

"Betsey! The baby's coming! Get the matron . . . I need help!" Flori gasped.

Anxiously, Betsey stumbled around sleeping bodies in the dark, over to where the matron slept near the prison door. Quickly, the matron lit a candle and hurried back with Betsey to Flori's side.

"Easy now, girl," said the matron. "Women give birth all the time. You're going to be all right." The matron's soothing voice kept up a running singsong, hoping to put the panting girl at ease.

But the baby didn't come. An hour went by, then two. Flori was drenched with sweat in the chilly prison room, her hair plastered around her face as she clenched her teeth, then panted and moaned. Betsey tried to dry her off with a corner of their blanket.

The matron frowned in the flickering lamplight. "Something's not right," she murmured. "We need a doctor or a midwife."

A large, dark shape moved toward the lamplight. "I'm a midwife."

Betsey jumped. It was Kitty Blunt—old Bixby's friend. Ever since Bixby had been taken away to the hanging cells, Kitty Blunt and Sally Webb had pretty much kept to themselves, sullenly working with the others in the prison workroom, but not causing any trouble, either.

"You?" the matron said, startled. "I didn't know—"

"Quit talking, woman," said Kitty gruffly. "The girl's in trouble. Let me see her."

The matron and Betsey stepped back. Kitty Blunt examined Flori, then swore. "The baby's in the wrong position," she muttered. "Hold that lamp higher!" she ordered the matron.

By now, most of the prisoners were awake and

crowding around to see what was happening. The mothers made clucking noises and offered advice, often contradicting each other, until Kitty Blunt's crusty voice ordered everyone to stand back and give them room.

Frightened, Betsey huddled against the wall. She tried to pray, but the only prayer she knew was the one Mrs. Fry had taught them: "Whate'er I do in anything, to do it as to Thee." Finally she just kept pleading over and over, "Help Flori, Jesus! Oh, help her, Jesus!"

The gray light of dawn was seeping into the prison yard when Kitty suddenly cried out gleefully, "The baby's turned! Now push, Flori . . . push!"

Flori uttered several long, agonized cries, then fell back, exhausted, against the matron's arms. In the silence that followed, Betsey heard a tiny, weak cry.

"A girl child," she heard Kitty mutter.

Snatching up the little patchwork quilt Flori had made, Betsey pushed close to the two women who were still busily tending to Flori and the baby. After a few minutes, to Betsey's astonishment, Kitty abruptly handed the tiny, naked infant to her, then the big woman turned her attention back to Flori, who was moaning on the straw mat.

Betsey quickly wrapped the soft, cotton quilt around the baby. She had a small, delicate face with a bow-shaped mouth and was waving one tiny fist in the air. "Aren't you beautiful!" Betsey whispered, awestruck—ignoring for the moment that the baby had not yet been washed and cleaned up after the birth.

But something was wrong with Flori. "This

woman needs a doctor," Kitty muttered to the matron. "Go quickly, woman!"

The matron hurried off to call someone to go for the prison doctor. But who knew how soon *he* would come?

"I . . . I want to see my baby," Flori called out weakly.

Betsey kneeled down on the floor by the straw mat and laid the bundle in Flori's arms. "A little girl," she said softly, beaming.

But to Betsey's surprise, tears ran down Flori's face. "Oh, little one . . . I didn't want to bring you into the world like this . . . in this awful place," she whispered. "We were supposed to be a family, you and me and . . . and . . ." Flori shook with fresh sobs.

"Come, come now," said Kitty Blunt gruffly. "Don't get yourself all upset. You need to rest." She bent to take the baby.

"Wait!" Flori said, clasping the baby to her. "I have to talk to Betsey."

"What is it, Flori?" Betsey said. She felt anxious, afraid. Flori was acting so strangely.

Flori reached out and grabbed Betsey's arm. "I want you to promise me that . . . if anything happens to me, you'll . . ."

"Don't!" Betsey said. "Stop talking like that, Flori. Nothing's going to happen to you."

"Promise me, Betsey," Flori gasped, weakly, "that you'll take care of the baby, as if she was your very own little sister."

Betsey pulled back, alarmed. What was Flori saying? How could she take care of a baby? She was only thirteen! And besides, she still hadn't given up the idea of getting herself sentenced to be transported to Botany Bay. What other future did she have? If she didn't get sentenced this time at her trial, why, there might still be time to do something. But a baby? A baby would spoil everything!

"Promise me, Betsey!" Flori demanded, her pretty face pinched with pain and exhaustion. Her hand remained clenched on Betsey's arm.

"F-Flori, I c-can't," Betsey stammered.

"Promise me!"

Betsey felt bewildered. What was Flori wanting her to do? She was delirious, that's what. But Flori was going to get better. She'd be all right soon.

"Promise me!"

"All—all right, Flori," Betsey finally said anxiously. "Don't worry. I'll take care of the baby."

Flori's hand released Betsey's arm and she fell back on the straw mat. "Take her now," she whispered weakly, holding the bundle out toward Betsey. "She'll be all right with you."

Trembling, Betsey took the baby from Flori and looked into the small face. The baby was sucking on her fist and making little whimpering sounds.

"The kid needs to feed," Kitty Blunt said, frowning. "Go 'round the yard, see if one of the mothers who is still nursing an infant will nurse this one, too."

Chapter 11

The Trial

MRS. FRY WAS VISIBLY UPSET when she arrived that morning and found Flori too weak and ill to sit up and eat her breakfast of prison mush after the difficult childbirth.

"Where is that doctor!" she fumed, pacing angrily back and forth. "Barbaric prison system, keeping a woman about to give birth locked up in the common prison yard with no medical attention. There ought to be a law!"

She paused. The matron was trying to spoon some food into Flori's mouth.

"Forgive my harsh words, matron," she said. "Thee acted nobly under the circumstances. And *thee*, Kitty Blunt," she said, turning gratefully to the tall woman who hovered nearby, "God bless thee for tending to Flori with thy midwifery skills. I have judged thee wrongly in the past. Forgive me."

"Huh!" Kitty Blunt snorted. "You judged me true enough. And don't thank me yet; the poor girl may not make it." She shook her head, muttering to herself. "If something goes wrong, you can always blame the midwife—everybody else does. That's why I'm rotting in Newgate, ain't it? Couldn't save the life of a spoiled rich lady who starved herself so she could be *thin*—never mind that she shoulda been eatin' fer two."

Betsey also sat nearby keeping an anxious eye on Flori as she held the baby who now slept peacefully—thanks to a fellow prisoner with a suckling child who willingly agreed to nurse the newborn.

Mrs. Fry looked at the watch she wore on a locket. "Oh, dear! It's time for Betsey's trial—and the doctor's not here yet! Still, we must do what must be done. Come, Betsey," she said, her voice softening. "It's time to go. I will go with thee."

Mechanically, Betsey gave the baby to Kitty Blunt, then bent close to Flori. "I'm going now, Flori, but don't worry. I'll be back soon," she whispered. "Everything's going to be all right. You just rest and get better, all right?" Then she walked slowly toward the prison door with Elizabeth Fry on one side and the matron on the other.

The courtroom serving Newgate Prison had a large gallery for spectators. But no one knew—or cared—about the trial of two homeless pickpockets, so the room was mostly empty. As Betsey sat on the stiff, hard bench in the prisoner's dock between her two supporters, she watched the judge arrive in powdered wig and black robe, followed by the local magistrate. Then the thief-catcher sauntered in, grinning, followed by the gentleman who'd had his wallet stolen. The latter looked impatient and cross at missing another half day of business.

Someone else sat down in the prisoner's dock. Betsey glanced up, then caught her breath. *Loren!* Her brother looked pale and thin, but he caught her eye and grinned. Betsey felt like jumping up and throwing her arms around her brother. How good it was to see him! But a frowning look from the matron forced her to look straight ahead and keep silent.

The judge's gavel banged on the great desk to call the court to order. The magistrate began by questioning the thief-catcher and the victim, in which they repeated the statements they'd made the day the two children had been arrested.

Betsey had a hard time paying attention. This was the day all prisoners both hoped for and dreaded—an end to the tedious months of waiting in prison and an answer to the fearful question, "What will be my fate?" But except for the excitement she felt at seeing Loren, her mind kept wandering back to the women's yard. Had the doctor come? Could he help Flori? What was going to happen to her and the baby?

"Do the prisoners have anything to say?" the

judge asked when all the evidence had been presented. Betsey just looked at the toes of her shoes. What was there to say? They did it, they got caught, they would get punished.

"Yes, Your honor, I do," said Loren's voice, loudly

and clearly. Startled, Betsey looked up. "I just want to make it clear before the court that I alone was responsible for what happened that day," he said. "My sister knew nothing about my plan to pick-pocket people in Tyburn Square. I was the one who hid the stolen wallets in her skirt pocket, and she allowed them to remain there only to keep me from getting in trouble."

No! No! Betsey wanted to cry out. *We did it together! Whatever happens to Loren should happen to me, too!*

"Does anyone else have anything to say?" the judge asked dryly.

"Yes, Your Honor, I do," said Elizabeth Fry, standing up respectfully. She made an imposing figure standing tall and straight in her white Quaker bonnet and plain gray dress. "I pray that the court will be merciful when sentencing these two unfortunate children, who, as orphans, had no moral guidance. I have long been concerned about young girls like Betsey Maxwell here who get caught up in crime without knowing what they are doing. Should they be kept in prison, just to keep them off the streets? God forbid! For here in prison they rub shoulders with every kind of wanton woman and criminal. But what happens to them when they are thrust back onto the streets? The temptation to break the law simply to survive sends many of these unfortunate girls back to prison, with even greater consequences."

Betsey frowned. What was Mrs. Fry getting at? Let the judge pass the sentences and get it over with.

Then she'd know if she was getting transported with Flori or not. If not . . . well, she had some new ideas for how to get arrested again, this time for petty stealing.

Mrs. Fry wasn't finished. "On the other hand, Your Honor, if young, abandoned girls had a shelter that could be their home after prison to guard them against the evil lurking in the city's slums, while at the same time giving them discipline and skills to become productive citizens—"

"Mrs. Fry," said the judge, "what is your point?"

"Your Honor, the Ladies Newgate Committee and I are currently making plans for such a shelter, which we are calling the School of Discipline for Neglected Girls. If it please the court to be lenient with the accused prisoner, Betsey Maxwell, and sentence her to the School of Discipline in lieu of any other punishment, I will take full responsibility for her rehabilitation until she reaches the age of eighteen."

Betsey's mouth dropped open. What was she talking about? What about Loren?

The judge and the magistrate leaned together, arguing back and forth. Minutes stretched on. Finally the judge cleared his throat. "The court has reached a decision. For one Loren Maxwell, minor, charged with pickpocketing . . . guilty. Sentenced to seven years transportation."

Betsey turned anguished eyes toward Loren. She saw him suck in his breath. But he held steady.

"For one Betsey Maxwell, minor, charged with

being an accomplice in the act of pickpocketing . . . guilty. But the court chooses to be lenient and waive the sentence *with the condition* that the accused attend Mrs. Elizabeth Fry's School of Discipline until the age of eighteen."

Bang went the gavel. "Court dismissed."

Betsey immediately whirled toward Loren, but her brother was already being hustled away by a guard. "Loren!" she cried. "Wait!" Everything was happening too fast! She needed to talk to Loren! She needed to say goodbye! But he was gone.

Dejected, Betsey walked back down the long stone corridor to the women's yard, tears stinging her eyes. She felt angry. Mrs. Fry had gone too far with her meddling ways. The judge said she was guilty; maybe she would have been sentenced to transportation with Loren and Flori if Mrs. Fry hadn't come up with her stupid School of Discipline, or whatever it was. It sounded just like another prison to Betsey. Well, if Elizabeth Fry was expecting her to be grateful, the lady could just forget it.

A guard unlocked the wood and iron door and let Betsey and the two women back into the women's yard. Betsey hurried over to where she'd left Flori . . . but Flori wasn't there.

"Flori!" she cried, looking around the big room. Maybe Flori was feeling better. Maybe she got up to use the slop pot. Maybe—

"The doctor came," Kitty Blunt announced as Elizabeth Fry and the matron joined them. "He actually seemed worried about her—called for a litter to

117

take her to the prison infirmary."

"I must go to her," said Mrs. Fry. "Where's the child?"

Kitty jerked her head toward one of the mothers. "Getting a good meal."

"I want to go see Flori!" Betsey said, starting after Mrs. Fry.

"No, you need to stay here," said Kitty, planting her large body in Betsey's way. "For the baby. That's what Flori wants."

The matron was already calling for the guard to unlock the door for Mrs. Fry.

"Me?" Betsey said. "But I don't know how—"

"I'll help you," said a voice behind her. It was the teacher, Mary Conner. "And Kitty Blunt is a midwife; she knows what to do. We'll all do it together."

✧ ✧ ✧ ✧

Mrs. Fry didn't come the next day, or the next. But the women from the Ladies Newgate Committee brought some baby clothes and nappies for Flori's baby, and Kitty Blunt showed Betsey how to give the baby a bath. Betsey felt stiff and awkward caring for the infant, and she anxiously watched the door, hoping that Flori would come back any minute. Every few hours she took the baby to one of the nursing mothers who had agreed to take turns feeding the little motherless infant, but most of the time she spent walking up and down the yard with the baby wrapped in the patchwork blanket, or just sitting nearby while the baby slept.

She was lonely without Flori. Ever since the first night at Newgate Prison, Betsey had slept with Flori on the straw mattress, taking comfort from the nearness of another human being. Flori was the one who showed her how to survive in prison and protected her from old Bixby. Flori was the person she confided in, who was always there to ask about Betsey's lessons after the Newgate School got started, who knew all about Betsey's mother and Loren and the workhouse.

At times, watching the sleeping baby, Betsey felt a stab of resentment tighten her heart. If the baby hadn't been born, Flori wouldn't be sick right now. Then, seeing the tiny eyelids flutter or the little mouth make sucking motions, Betsey felt ashamed. "It's not your fault, little one," she whispered, picking up the baby and cuddling it close to her. "You want your mama as much as I do. For one thing, she needs to give you a name! We can't call you 'Flori's baby' the rest of your life."

The third day Elizabeth Fry returned to the prison yard. She looked tired and downcast. As the anxious prisoners gathered around, she said simply, "Flori died last night. An infection . . . fever. She was simply too weak to fight it."

Betsey felt as though the breath had been knocked out of her. *No!* Flori couldn't—! Not Flori! She stood as if rooted to the floor, unable to cry or feel.

Time seemed to slow. Betsey sank to the floor. Flori dead? Nothing was happening like it was supposed to happen. Nothing in her life ever worked out. Betsey's mind drifted, as if in a trance, over everything that had happened in the last three years . . . her mother's arrest and exile . . . the workhouse . . . Loren picking pockets at Tyburn Square . . . Newgate Prison . . . her scheme to get herself transported with Flori—

A tiny cry broke the trance. Betsey looked down at the baby she was still holding, its delicate face screwed up in an unhappy cry. Betsey blinked. The baby. What about the baby? And suddenly she was breathing hard. What if her scheme *had* worked? What if she had gotten herself transported and then Flori died? The baby would be alone with no one to take care of her!

Around her women were talking in low undertones or weeping quietly. "We must find a foster home for the baby," Mrs. Fry was saying. "I will ask around—"

"No!" Betsey heard herself saying. She stood up.

"What's that, Betsey?" Mrs. Fry said.

"You don't need to find a foster family," Betsey said, her voice shaking. Were those words really coming out of her mouth? "She's my little sister now. Flori said so."

"Why, of course," Mrs. Fry said sympathetically. "I understand how you feel. You and Flori were very close. But, it's really quite impossible. The baby is an orphan now, and we need to find a family who will—"

"The kid's right," Kitty Blunt spoke up. "Flori made Betsey promise that she would take care of the baby if, well, if anything happened to her."

"Well, I . . ." Flustered, Elizabeth Fry looked at the matron for help.

But the matron slowly nodded her head. "It's true, Mrs. Fry. I heard Flori make Betsey promise. It's what Flori wanted."

"But . . . but Betsey will be going to the School of Discipline for Neglected Girls as soon as it gets started," Mrs. Fry protested. "The judge said so. A baby just won't fit in with the plans for the school."

Kitty Blunt grinned. "It will if you want it to, Mrs. Fry. I ain't never seen anything yet that you wanted to happen that didn't get done somehow."

There were sympathetic chuckles around the group of women prisoners.

Tears slid down Betsey's cheeks and dropped on the patchwork bundle in her arms. "The baby has a name now," she whispered, looking down at the sleeping baby. "Her mother was Flori Alexander. Flori means *flower*. So I'm going to call her baby Daisy—Daisy Alexander Maxwell."

And finally, Betsey cried.

Chapter 12

The Hope

"Betsey?" Elizabeth Fry peeked into the school-room of the School of Discipline. "Can thee spare a minute?"

Betsey looked up from her schoolwork. In a corner of the large, sunny room, a volunteer from the Ladies Newgate Committee was rocking six-month-old Daisy so that Betsey could concentrate on her studies.

She and Daisy had been living at the school for four months now. Mrs. Fry had found another wet nurse who could feed the baby until the baby could be weaned to goat's milk. Other

young girls from the prison, ranging in age from eight to eighteen, had also been "sentenced" to the school at Mrs. Fry's persuasion. So far there were five girls in addition to a matron, head housekeeper, and teacher—not to mention an impressive list of volunteers who came in to teach the girls various skills—but Mrs. Fry wouldn't be happy until the large house that sheltered the school was full of twenty to thirty neglected girls.

The girls were given a small allowance, which they were supposed to budget for their own clothing and food. They took turns planning meals, doing the daily shopping, and doing the household chores under the supervision of the housekeeper. Betsey was learning how to sew, besides reading, writing, arithmetic, and science. All the girls grumbled about the disciplined schedule, which included prayers, meals, work, studies, exercise, and regular rest. But four months of this regime had put weight back on Betsey's thin body and color in her cheeks, and the nagging cough was finally gone.

Little Daisy was thriving, too. Everyone was crazy about the pretty baby, and Mrs. Fry declared that the child would never learn to crawl at this rate because there was always a pair of arms eager to pick her up and play with her. She was a good-natured baby, and a smile and giggle from Daisy usually cheered anyone who showed up for meals or lessons in a sour mood. But it was also obvious that Betsey was the center of Daisy's universe, and the two were inseparable.

In fact, Betsey would have been fairly happy at the School of Discipline if it wasn't for the loneliness of missing Flori, and for worrying about when Loren was going to be transported.

Seeing Mrs. Fry in the schoolroom doorway, Betsey got a nod from the teacher and slipped quietly out of the room. "Do you have any word from Newgate?" she asked anxiously.

Elizabeth Fry nodded. "The convict ships arrived at the docks today. It will take them at least a week to do repairs, restock supplies, and get a new crew. As soon as I hear when the actual sailing date has been set, I will let thee know, Betsey."

"Who . . . is on the list to be transported?"

Mrs. Fry took a deep breath. "Among the men, Loren is the only one I know, although there are probably eighty or so from Newgate—more from other prisons around England. Among the women, well, thee knows about Mrs. Ripley—"

"What about Sissy and the other children?" Betsey asked anxiously.

"Mrs. Ripley is taking the two youngest with her. Sissy and the oldest boy will be staying with their father—a decent man who has given up drink and is trying to make the best of a heart-wrenching situation."

"Go on."

Mrs. Fry named as many of the women as she could remember. "The list includes Kitty Blunt and Sally Webb," she concluded.

"What about Mary Conner?" Betsey asked anxiously. She'd heard the prison teacher's trial date had been set, but her name wasn't on the list to be transported. Betsey felt a stab of alarm. Surely Mary Conner of all people had not been sentenced to—

"That's the good news!" Mrs. Fry smiled. "Mary Conner was pardoned by the judge for her positive contribution to the welfare of prisoners at Newgate Prison." The smile faded. "Although . . ." She hesitated.

"What's the matter?" Betsey asked.

"She's not well," Mrs. Fry admitted. "She developed a cough soon after you left and . . . and recently she's been spitting up blood."

"Consumption?" Betsey said, eyes wide. In her experience, all fourteen years of it, people usually died from consumption sooner or later.

"We must pray it isn't so," said Mrs. Fry soberly. "But thee must know, dear Betsey, if Mary dies, it will be we who are sad—not she. For she now believes on Jesus, and even though her body has not yet left Newgate Prison, her spirit is already free."

Betsey turned slowly and went back into the schoolroom, her heart heavy. Why even bother loving someone? It seemed as though everyone she really cared for either died or went away.

The other girls were gathering up their books and slates; study time was over. Baby Daisy spotted Betsey and held out her arms happily. Betsey took the baby from the volunteer and smiled in spite of herself. "Except for you, Daisy Alexander Maxwell," she murmured, rubbing noses with the baby and making Daisy laugh. As she walked Daisy back to the cubbyhole room she and the baby shared, she whispered fiercely in the tiny ear, "And I promise you, little sister, I will *never* do anything that would get me put back into Newgate Prison."

❖ ❖ ❖ ❖

Betsey bundled Daisy in a warm sweater and knitted cap, wrapped the patchwork quilt around her, and went outside to the waiting carriage. It was a crisp fall day, sunny for this time of year, but the wind was brisk. Today was the day the prisoners would be taken to the docks to board the convict ships, and Mrs. Fry had promised she could see Loren once more.

But as the driver slapped the reins on the backs of the horses, she dreaded what lay ahead. In her mind's eye, she remembered the open wagons of terrified prisoners and the jeering, hostile crowd harassing her mother all the way from the prison to the docks.

Shaking her head, she tried to chase away the memory. She didn't dare think about it, or she'd lose her courage. She glanced at Elizabeth Fry who sat opposite her, playing peekaboo with Daisy.

"You spend an awful lot of time with criminals," Betsey said suddenly. "Don't your own children miss you?"

A pained look crossed Mrs. Fry's face, then was gone. "My boys are gone away to school," she said, "and my older girls are spending the winter months with their aunts and uncles. Only the three little ones are at home—and yes, they don't see enough of their mama, though they have a wonderful nanny who cares for them."

"But why do you leave them to spend time in *prison*? I wouldn't go there—not if the thief-catcher hadn't put me there."

"Because right now the mothers and children in Newgate need me, too." Elizabeth Fry smiled. "It has always seemed to me that we who consider ourselves God's servants must be prepared to do part of God's work. And the Bible tells us to bear one another's burdens." She glanced out the carriage window at the passing buildings. "But I couldn't do it without the support of my dear husband, Joe Fry."

Betsey started to ask if he was the man she had seen with Mrs. Fry the day her mother was transported—but just then the carriage rumbled through the gate to Newgate Prison and into the big stone-paved courtyard.

"Stay in the carriage," Mrs. Fry cautioned as she got out and went over to speak to some prison officials. Betsey peered out the carriage window. Why were there so many carriages in the prison courtyard today? Were they going to get to see Loren here? Or would they have to drive down to the dock? Would she get to speak to him, or—

Daisy started to fuss, and Betsey rubbed the little gums where teeth were starting to poke through in the way the wet nurse had showed her. But Daisy soon let loose with a full-blown cry.

The carriage door opened and a voice said, "Well, that's not quite the welcome I expected."

"Loren!" Betsey cried. He climbed into the coach, wrists and ankles free of irons. This time Betsey did throw her arms around him and held him in a long hug. "Oh, Loren," she whispered. Daisy stopped crying as Betsey started.

"Hey, now, don't cry," Loren chided gently. "We don't have enough time for that."

Elizabeth Fry climbed back into the carriage and shut the door. Through the window Betsey could see other prisoners getting into the closed carriages, and she caught glimpses of joyful family reunions. In astonishment she looked at Mrs. Fry. "No open wagons? Families ride together? How did you manage that?"

Mrs. Fry smiled. "God opened the doors. I just knocked on a few." She pulled the window curtains.

Betsey and Loren barely noticed when the carriage pulled out of the courtyard and rolled through the streets of London toward the docks on the River Thames. "Oh, Loren," Betsey said, "I should be going with you. We should be going together so you wouldn't be alone."

He shook his head. "We'd be together about as much as we've been 'together' in Newgate Prison," he said wryly. "The men travel on one ship; the women on another. Besides," he lifted Daisy from Betsey's arms and settled the curious baby on his lap, "you've got somebody who needs you more than I do now."

He touched Daisy's soft, wispy curls.

They rode in silence for a few moments. Then Loren said, "Maybe this is for the best, Betsey— going to Botany Bay, I mean. I've thought a lot about it. Maybe I'll find our mother there and can help her. After all, she was only sentenced to seven years exile . . ."

"Very few ever come back," Mrs. Fry reminded him gently.

"I know that!" he said, hitting the seat cushion with his fist. "But . . . maybe if she had a strong lad like me to work, to earn our passage home. Maybe someday . . ."

"Oh, Loren, if you only could!" Betsey breathed. It was something to hope for—it wasn't wrong to hope, was it? She looked at her brother with affection. He was only sixteen, she realized, but nine months in prison made him seem much older.

Suddenly Loren turned to Elizabeth Fry. "How can I ever thank you, Mrs. Fry, for giving Betsey a real chance! If . . . if I had to go and leave Betsey behind out on the streets, easy prey for every pimp and drunk sailor and thief wantin' to make a shilling, why—" Loren stopped, overcome with emotion.

Daisy reached up and pulled on Loren's nose, making everyone laugh.

Loren took a deep breath. "But," he went on, "knowing that Betsey, and little Daisy here, are at the school with you, why, they can ship me to Botany Bay or Devil's Island or wherever they like, 'cause now I have peace of mind."

Mrs. Fry touched his arm gently. "No, Loren, true peace only comes when God dwells within thee."

He gave a short, bitter laugh. "I don't think I have the grace to be a Quaker—love your enemies, turn the other cheek, plain clothes, and all that."

She smiled. "Not everyone is called to be a Quaker. But everyone *is* called to receive God the Savior. Think on it while thee travels long months on the sea. And take this with thee." She rummaged in her bag and handed him a large, well-used book. Betsey's eyes widened. It looked just like Mrs. Fry's own Bible.

They rode quietly the last half mile to the dock. Carriage after carriage rumbled out onto the dock, and suddenly the prisoners and their families were saying goodbye. Loren shook Mrs. Fry's hand, then gave Betsey and little Daisy a fierce hug . . . and then he was gone, up the gangplank of the convict ship with the other prisoners.

Betsey shifted Daisy to her other hip and shaded her eyes against the midday sun. Her heart ached, but somehow she also felt a glimmer of hope in the middle of her sadness. This wasn't goodbye; not for forever. Something linked them that was stronger than distance across large oceans.

Maybe it was the Bible that Mrs. Fry had given to Loren. Maybe it was Loren's promise that he would try to find their mother.

But for some reason, Betsey knew that someday they would be together again.

More About Elizabeth Fry

JOHN GURNEY, ESQUIRE, and his wife, Catherine, both came from Quaker families, known as the Society of Friends, and raised their children as nominal Quakers near the town of Norwich, Norfolk County, England. Elizabeth, the third daughter, born May 21, 1780, was not particularly religious as a child, often scolding herself in her journal for her lack of "religious feeling."

The Gurneys were a banking family, enjoying middle-class wealth at Earlham, their country home about two miles from Norwich. But the Gurney family raised their children with a social conscience. Elizabeth's younger brother John refused for a time to take any sugar in his tea, because of the "poor slaves" (slave labor was used to raise sugar cane).

Elizabeth was rather sickly as a child and a bit of a loner, writing intimately in her journal. As one sister expressed it, she seemed "to have no one for a friend, for none of us are intimate with her." Of twelve brothers and sisters, she was closest to Rachel, the second oldest daughter, and her younger brother John Gurney.

In 1792, when Elizabeth was twelve, her mother Catherine died, leaving eleven living children from age two to seventeen. The oldest girls became responsible for caring for the younger children and managing the family home. They also continued their mother's example of giving aid to their poorer neighbors. But like young people in all times and places, they longed for parties and good times and pretty clothes and often grumbled about the two-hour-long silent Quaker "meetings."

But in 1798, at the age of eighteen, Elizabeth attended special meetings to hear the American Quaker, William Savery, speak. Her heart was strangely moved, and that night she wrote in her journal, "Today I have felt that there is a God."

From that time on, Elizabeth developed a deepening conviction about spiritual things. In the summer of that same year, she heard and was much influenced by another Quaker preacher, this time a woman named Deborah Darby. By the next year she had decided to become a "Plain Friend"—a branch of the Quakers who underscored basic Quaker beliefs in the simplicity of life and the brotherhood of all people by giving up worldly amusements and adopting the plain Quaker dress.

This was quite a transformation for a girl who had previously gone about the neighborhood delivering food baskets to the poor dressed in a scarlet riding habit—and her sisters thought she was taking this "spiritual thing" a bit too seriously. One of Elizabeth's concerns were the children around Norwich whose parents were too poor to send them to school. She began tutoring them, and her school, known among the neighbors as "Betsey's Imps," grew to seventy children.

A young man named Joseph Fry, also a Plain Friend, was quite attracted by this serious and handsome young woman. Elizabeth and Joseph were married in 1800 and left dear Earlham to move to St. Mildred's Court, the Fry family home, which was attached to the family's place of business—importing tea, which later expanded into banking, probably due to Gurney family influence. Though Elizabeth dearly loved her husband and soon gave birth to the first of eleven children, she was restless and often felt she was not "doing enough" to fulfill her religious obligations.

As mistress of St. Mildred's Court, she read the Bible daily to her servants, was generous in their salary, and felt it was her duty to "make them happy in their station in life." Never feeling the pinch of poverty herself, her attitude toward wealth was "a fine Christian simplicity"—meaning an "austere luxury," or "good quality" simplicity. All her life she was generous with her income to care for others as well as see to the needs of her own family.

Soon after her marriage, she became acquainted with Joseph Lancaster's school in Southwark and was impressed by the Lancastrian or monitorial system of instruction, in which children were divided into smaller teams, assisted by a monitor, which enabled a single teacher to teach a larger number of students. This was later to influence her prison work.

After the death of Joseph's father in 1808, the Fry family was able to move to Plashet, the Fry country home, at least during the summer. This was deeply refreshing to Elizabeth's spirit. She had missed the country air, flowers, and gardens of her childhood home at Earlham.

A woman who used her private journal as a "spiritual friend," Elizabeth was usually quite shy in public. However, at the age of twenty-nine she felt moved by the Spirit to speak up in a Quaker meeting and share her spiritual insights. The other members were quite astonished at first, but also recognized that her words ministered truth to the assembly—and within two years, Elizabeth Gurney Fry had been officially acknowledged as a Quaker minister. She was never quite comfortable with the role, but she also felt spiritual urgency from within to serve God in whatever capacity He laid before her. At various times during her lifetime, this meant making journeys around England with other Quaker ministers to visit various meetings and encourage the believers.

Whether in London or at Plashet, Elizabeth's heart was always turned toward the poor. In her closets she kept a large supply of calico, warm flannels, and medicines to distribute to families in need. During the winter her servants were instructed to boil up a large pot of soup each day to help feed the hungry.

In 1812, a Quaker named Stephen Grellet visited Newgate Prison. The appalling conditions for both men and women prisoners prompted him to inform Elizabeth Fry. Soon after, she visited the women's prison inside Newgate one or two times, taking along warm garments, and was shaken to see three hundred women and children crammed into several small rooms and a narrow yard. The women lived, cooked, and washed all in the same area—old and young, tried and untried, women accused of violent crimes and petty thieves. They were a hard lot, swearing, swigging beer, singing lewd songs, chewing and spitting tobacco just like their male counterparts. With few creature comforts, the women shamelessly begged money from visitors, often using it to buy gin from the prison tap room to drown their sorrows.

Pressing family concerns—several illnesses, the birth of one child, the death of another—kept Elizabeth Fry away from Newgate for several years. But in February, 1817, she returned. At each visit she simply talked with the women and read the Scriptures to them. But soon she had established a school for the "poor innocent children" locked up with their mothers, as well as younger criminals, sometimes girls no older than seven. One of the pressing needs of the women was simply "something to do"—with too much idle time on their hands, they turned to drink and fighting.

In April of that year, the wife of a clergyman and eleven members of the Society of Friends, with the help of Elizabeth Fry, formed "An Association for the Improvement of the Female Prisoners in Newgate," often just referred to as the Ladies Newgate Committee. The purpose of this group was:

1. To provide clothing
2. To provide instruction
3. To provide employment
4. To introduce knowledge of Holy Scriptures
5. To form habits of order, sobriety, and industry "to render them docile and peaceable while in prison and respectable when they leave it."

One of the ladies on the committee had the idea that the prisoners could supply articles of clothing for Botany Bay, the prison colony for exiles in New South Wales—part of what we know today as Australia. Mrs. Fry went to Messrs. Richard Dizon and Co., of Fenchurch Street, saying she wanted to "deprive them of this branch of their trade"; surprisingly, they cooperated with her, telling her to bring them finished products from the prison, which they would then sell.

With a market for the women's work, the prison laundry was turned into a workroom, and Elizabeth turned her attention to organizing the women within the prison. Her attitude in working with the women was always "we"—not "you." It was not in her nature to command, expecting the prisoners to obey. Rather she desired that all should act in agreement. No rule was made or monitor appointed without their full and unanimous approval. If someone had a disagreement, she was invited to voice her objection.

The Ladies Committee also appointed a matron of the prison. The prisoners were divided into classes and placed under the matron's oversight.

Later that same spring, she arranged a meeting with the Governor of the Prison, a Mr. Newman, the chaplain, other officials, the prisoners, and the Ladies Committee. When the officials saw what was happening in the prison, they made it an official part of the prison system at Newgate.

While not directly challenging the system, Elizabeth worked from within to treat prisoners more humanely. One of her concerns was the deplorable treatment of prisoners sentenced to "transportation"—i.e., exile to the port city of Botany Bay in New South Wales. There was often a riot in the prison the night prior to sailing. The next morning, prisoners in chains were carted to the docks in open wagons, accompanied by heckling, jeering crowds. The British mentality at this time was to simply get rid of the so-called criminal class and dump them on the other side of the world.

In the summer of 1818, Mrs. Fry arranged for the prisoners to be taken to the docks in closed carriages, accompanied by their families. From then until 1840, she visited every female transport ship leaving England for New South Wales. On ship, too, she organized the prisoners, arranged for the teaching of the children and productive work to do. Admiral Sir Byam Martin was Comptroller of the Navy from 1813–1832; many improvements in the transportation of criminals took place under his direction because of the influence of Elizabeth Fry.

In 1819, at the age of thirty-nine, Elizabeth became pregnant for the eleventh time, but she miscarried. It was her last pregnancy. She had given birth to ten children, one of whom died at age five. Nine children grew to adulthood, most of whom married outside the Quaker faith.

In the early 1820s, Elizabeth helped establish several "asylums" or shelters for released prisoners, where they could learn new skills and become productive citizens. One of these was a home "for vicious and neglected little girls," ages seven to thirteen, convicted of stealing, which was opened at Chelsea.

Elizabeth Fry was also responsible for founding District Visiting Societies, similar to the Ladies Newgate Committee, in other cities and towns all over England, for the improvement of prisons in each district.

In 1829, Joseph Fry experienced the failure of the family bank. The financial crisis forced him to sell Plashet, their country home. At this time, Elizabeth Fry, up till now considered the "wonder woman" of prison reform, was also beginning to receive a lot of criticism. Had she made prison life "too comfortable" for criminals? Her opponents argued that harsh prison life was a deterrent to criminal activity. But Mrs. Fry continued to work for reform, including opposing capital punishment for crimes such as stealing and forgery, and solitary confinement as a punishment which, she said, "broke the spirit" rather than reformed the person.

All during these years, Elizabeth Fry continued to write in her journals. She gave only passing mention to major events and honors such as her audience with Queen Victoria of England; rather her journals were filled with her spiritual thoughts and struggles, concerns for loved ones, and the spiritual philosophy of life she continued to develop and refine.

Early in her life, Elizabeth had developed six rules for herself:

1. Never lose any time; I do not think that lost which is spent in amusement or recreation, some time every day; but always be in the habit of being employed.
2. Never err the least in truth.
3. Never say an ill thing of a person when I can say a good thing of him or her; not only speak charitably, but feel so.
4. Never be irritable nor unkind to anybody.
5. Never indulge myself in luxuries that are not necessary.
6. Do all things in consideration, and when my path to right is most difficult, feel confidence in that Power that alone is able to assist me, and exert my own powers as far as they go.

Though she was not always in good health and had many family responsibilities to fulfill, Elizabeth Fry continued to reach out to those less fortunate than herself for the sake of Christ. Her prayer until her death in 1845, at the age of sixty-five, was always, "Whate'er I do in any thing, to do it as to Thee."

For Further Reading

Rose, June. *Elizabeth Fry.* London: Macmillan, 1980.

Cresswell, Francis. *A Memoir of Elizabeth Fry.* London: James Nisbet and Co., 1868. Abridged from the original, larger memoir by her daughter.

Whitney, Janet. *Elizabeth Fry—Quaker Heroine.* New York: Benjamin Blom, Inc., 1972.